CAFFEINE NIG

COLD
LONDON
BLUES

PAUL D. BRAZILL

Fiction aimed at the heart

and the head...

Published by Caffeine Nights Publishing 2016

Published in Great Britain by Caffeine Nights Publishing

www.caffeinenights.com

British Library Cataloguing in Publication Data.

A CIP catalogue record for this book is available from the British Library

ISBN: 978-1-910720-55-4

Cover design by
Mark (Wills) Williams

Everything else by
Default, Luck and Accident

Cold London Blues

Paul D. Brazill

For Peter Ord

Paul D. Brazill is the author of Cold London Blues, The Last Laugh, Guns Of Brixton, and Kill Me Quick! He was born in England and lives in Poland. He is an International Thriller Writers Inc member whose writing has been translated into Italian, German and Slovene. He has had writing published in various magazines and anthologies, including The Mammoth Books of Best British Crime. He has even edited a few anthologies, including the best-selling True Brit Grit.

Acknowledgments:

Darren E. Laws and all at Caffeine Nights Publishing. Vic Godard. Renato Bratkovic, Mark Hammonds. Catherine Hill. Peter Ord. Niki and Julian. Mam, dad, Sandra, Sonia, Brian, Eric. Daria and Dorian, Ula. Jason Michel, Richard Godwin, K A Laity. Les Edgerton. Aneta Uszynska. Oliver Robinson. Martin Stanley. Nigel Bird. Lesley Walsh. Dominic Milne. Kevin Tipple. Kasia Martell. Graham Smith. Maxim Jakubowski. Warren Stalley. Robert Cowan. Ryan Bracha. Keith Nixon. Chris Rhatigan. Chris Black. Marty and Tim Cook. Richard Sanderson. Keith Rawson. David Cranmer. Elaine Ash. Everyone whose names, anecdotes, jokes and lives I've borrowed. Colman Keane. Peter Rozovsky. Seana Graham. Crime Fiction Lover. Everyone who has read and enjoyed my stuff.

Contents

WATCHING THE DEVIL

The morning that Father Tim Cook killed Aldo Calvino the air tasted like lead and the sky was gun-metal grey.

'I tell you what, Aldo, I'm gagging for a smoke, a mug of slosh and a bacon sarnie smothered in brown sauce,' said Tim, scratching his newly shaven head. 'I think I'll pop into Madge's Mini Coffee Pot in a bit. If she's open, that is, what with it being New Year's Day. She was last year, mind you.'

Aldo groaned. His blubbery body was naked except for a blood-stained paisley dressing gown that was soaked in sweat. He was handcuffed to a rusty radiator, and panting like a wounded mongrel.

'She does a good fry-up, does Madge, eh?' said Tim.

Aldo mumbled to himself.

'Yeah,' said Tim. 'I suspect you've lost your appetite. Better late than never, eh?'

He winked.

Aldo grunted. Looked constipated. Croaked like a frog.

'Tim, Tim, please …'

The words tumbled out of his flabby mouth like a gang of drunks staggering out of a pub at closing time; disorderly and unruly. He begged, he pleaded, argued, cajoled, screamed, threatened, but it was all to no avail, of course. It was just white noise in the background to Father Tim who turned away and looked out of the window of Aldo's flat, barely focusing on the rows of concrete blocks that were being smudged by the early morning rain.

He edged through the obstacle course of junk and out onto the balcony to have a smoke. He looked out across the London skyline. The inky-black night had melted into a grubby-grey January morning. The city was waking now and the windows of the other granite tower blocks outside were starting to light up.

A cold wind, as sharp as a razor blade, sliced through him and Father Tim fastened his leather biker's jacket as tightly as possible. Dark, malignant clouds crawled ominously across the sky.

'Pissin' miserable weather,' he muttered to himself. 'Pissin' miserable country.'

He took a crushed packet of Marlborough cigarettes from the back pocket of his Levis, fished inside with shaking fingers.

On the opposite balcony, a tall man with long black hair took breadcrumbs from a plastic bag and threw them in the air. Black birds darted down from telephone lines where they had been lined up like notes on sheet music. The birds flew towards the tall man, landing on his balcony and sometimes on him. His raucous, joyous laughter brought an unfamiliar smile to Father Tim's face.

On the street below, he could see a branch of a small general dealers with a bright green logo above the door, as well as an old bicycle factory that had recently been converted into a Wetherspoons pub, and a stretch of hip bars, including Noola's Saloon, its green neon sign flickering intermittently.

The street bustled with the drunken debris of the previous night's New Year's Eve parties. The still pissed and the newly hungover mingled. A massive skinhead in a leopard skin coat walked up to Noola's Saloon and pressed a door bell. The door opened emitting a screech of escaping metallic music as he slipped inside. Iggy and The Stooges' *Search and Destroy*. A sense of longing enveloped Father Tim. A feeling of time passing like grains of sand through his fingers.

Father Tim felt his rheumatism bite as he inhaled his first cigarette of the day. His chest felt heavy. If ever there was time to get the hell out of London it was probably now. The quack had told him to piss off to Spain, or somewhere as sunny, for a bit, for his health's sake. It wasn't a bad idea, either. He could even stay at his sister-in-law's gaff in Andalucía if he wanted. But he knew he wouldn't stay away for long. London was in his bones. His blood. His lungs. For better or for worse.

As he finished the cancer stick, lightning flashed, thunder boomed and the heavens were gutted. Tim stepped back inside and closed the rickety window.

'Ey, Aldo, did you hear the one about the young bird that comes back from her holidays in Lansagrotty and tells her mum she thinks she's pregnant?' said Father Tim 'Her mum's shocked and says "Have you had a check-up?" and the bird says "No I think he was Polish?"'

He turned to Aldo and grinned.

'Get it? Check-up/ *Czech up*?'

Aldo shook his head.

'Suit yourself?' said Tim.

Aldo ignored him and stared at the threadbare carpet. Licked his lips.

'You know the thing about life, Aldo? The thing about life is that you can't rely on anyone, can you?' said Tim. 'You're on your own in this life. A lone boat adrift on a sea of meaninglessness and chaos, eh?'

Aldo said nothing.

'Mork calling Orson,' said Tim. 'Is there anybody there? Knock once for yes, twice for no.' He leaned forward and tapped a fist on Aldo's sweaty forehead.

Aldo looked up, smiled weakly.

'Is ... is it closing time?' said Aldo.

Tim grinned.

'No time like the present,' said Tim.

The fat man started to sob and his head slumped forward onto his chest, his saggy jowls melding with his flabby torso.

Father Tim loomed over him.

'Dominus noster Jesus Christus te absolvat; et ego auctoritate ipsius te absolvo ab omni vinculo excommunicationis ...'said the priest, as he took his Bowie knife and plunged it into Aldo's heart, mercifully cutting short the man's pitiful, and quite annoying sobbing. 'Sic transit Gloria friggin' Gaynor'.

He twisted the blade until Aldo's life faded away, just like hot breath on a cold window pane. After a few moments, Tim pulled the Bowie knife free of the corpulent corpse, wiped its blade clean on the grubby lace curtains and pushed it into his shoulder holster. Tim wasn't usually a big fan of the Yanks, to be sure, but the US Army certainly knew how to make knives, he had to admit. Credit where credit was due.

He wriggled his stiff fingers to get some life back in them and trudged across the room. Looked in the grubby mirror that hung over a battered old sofa. Grunted.

The ghost of a particularly maudlin and gruelling Radiohead song drifted into the flat through a cracked window as Father Tim unsuccessfully used a thumb nail to try to scrape the splashes of blood from his dog collar, and he was immediately cloaked in gloom. He couldn't help but notice how old he was looking these days. A face so lived-in squatters wouldn't stay there, as his old gran would have said. His recent decision to shave his head hadn't exactly help matters either. He was looking like a ravaged bulldog.

He grunted again, yawned and stretched. He was completely knackered. It had been a right pain in the arse tracking down Aldo. Much more difficult than he'd thought. It had taken him most of the previous day to find the shithole of a flat, for example. Sunday friggin' Sunday. Day of rest, my arse, he thought.

He looked around Aldo's digs with disgust. Apparently, the previous owner was some has-been 1950s matinee idol who had croaked of a heroin overdose. Tim had never heard of the bloke and whether or not he had been responsible for what passed for the flat's interior design, Tim didn't know, but it truly was an abomination.

The joint was like a Hieronymus Bosch painting. A hodgepodge and mish-mash of particularly ugly second-hand furniture. The worst examples of every style and era seemed to have been paid lip service to with no thought of cohesion or style. Tim sighed. He'd quite liked Aldo, to be honest, but was appalled to see how the mighty had fallen. Once upon a time Aldo had been a big-shot fence living the life of Riley in some massive Edwardian gaff over in North London, with a tidy little Albino bint in tow. Unfortunately for him, he'd recently become a liability as far as Tim's Uncle Tony was concerned. A loose end that needed tying up and throwing in the bottom of a river.

Somehow or other, Aldo must have found out that Mad Tony Cook was ready to rub him out, though, and he'd done a runner, gone on the lam. AWOL. Ending up living in this shithole.

Father Tim looked back at Aldo's mangled body and checked his Rolex. He'd have to get that mess cleaned up sharpish or otherwise he wouldn't be able get back in time for *The Jeremy Kyle Show* – New Year's Day Special. He loved laughing at the idiots they had on that show and this one promised to be particularly cringe-worthy if the previews were anything to go by. Schadenfreude wasn't just a crap German wine.

There was an old black and white television in the corner of the room and he would have watched the show on that but it was showing yet another bloody cookery programme and Father Tim couldn't find the remote control to change channels. That fat-lipped boy with the counterfeit cockney accent was on the box again blabbing on about school dinners. Tim wasn't sure when it was that domestic drudgery like cooking and gardening had become elevated to the level of the works of Beethoven and Chaucer but it was another sign of what was wrong with the modern world, the country. A paucity of imagination.

He took out his Samsung Galaxy to send a text message his Uncle Tony but instead sat down in the sofa for a quick game of Flappy Birds and remembered that he really needed to upgrade his smartphone. It seemed like it was one thing after another these days, it really did.

His phone vibrated. He sighed and with Sisyphean resignation answered it.

'Morning Uncle Tony,' he said. 'And a happy New Year to you. What can I do you for?'

'Is it all over?' rasped Mad Tony Cook.

'It is now,' said Father Tim. 'Well, for Aldo, at any rate.'

'Good boy. Any news on Ron Moody?' said Tony.

'Not as such. He's gone completely underground by the looks of things. You never know, though,' said Tim 'Maybe somebody stuck a stake through his heart.'

Tony chuckled.

'You going to torch the place?' said Tony.

'No, not this one. No one will report the smell in this dump. I've got a couple of rat boys on the job,' said Tim. 'They're going to slice him up and sell his bits off to one of the trendy organic meat stalls down Borough market.'

'I've always been in favour of recycling,' said Tony. 'What goes around comes around.'

'Indeed.'

'Keep me in the loop,' said Tony.

'Will do,' said Tim.

Tony hung up and Tim sat for a moment listening to the sounds of the city. His city. At least it had been once upon a time. In many ways, he didn't recognise it these days. It was becoming homogenised corporate cobblers. Even Soho and Tin Pan Alley. Jeffrey Bernard must be spinning in his grave. A car pulled up outside the block playing Dillinger's *Cocaine In My Brain* loudly. There were shouts and then it skidded off. A few minutes later, there was a furtive knock at the door.

Tim creaked as he got to his feet and opened the door to two heavily pierced, snivelling, shuffling ratboys wearing identical black hoodies. Their red eyes glared out from sweaty, spotty, green tinged skin. They were almost identical in their appearance and movements, like a mad scientist's experiment gone badly wrong. Baghead Berry and Monkey Boy jumped back as soon as they saw Father Tim.

'Bless me father, for …,' said Monkey Boy, crossing himself.

'Yeah, whatever. There you go,' said Father Tim.

He handed Baghead Berry a key. 'Make sure to lock-up after you leave.'

'Will, do, will do,' said Monkey Boy. He looked into the flat and licked his lips.

Tim left the flat and headed down the stairs, unable to face the stink of the lift.

Out on the high street, the cold morning rain was refreshing. Liberating.

He stepped over a tattered and torn placard that proclaimed the imminent end of the world, shrugged, took off his dog collar and shoved it in his coat pocket. He felt the morning chill then.

As he walked past Black Jacks Casino, he noticed a couple of ruddy faced Champagne Charlies stagger out, swearing like troupers. One of them was wearing a particularly attractive paisley cravat. Tim stepped towards them.

'Spare a quid, guv,' said Tim, a fake tremor in his voice.

'Oh, for god's sake,' said the toff wearing the cravat. 'Kindly fuck off and die. I just can't …'

Tim jabbed him in the throat and punched him in the face.

'Hey!' said his friend, who grabbed Tim's arm.

Tim swiftly head-butted him and within minutes, he and his companion were on the rain soaked pavement, groaning with pain, blood bursting from their noses.

'And a merry Xmas to you, too,' said Father Tim, as he removed the cravat. 'Ho ho ho.'

He put on the cravat and sauntered down the street whistling Jona Lewie's *Stop The Cavalry*.

***

Be-Bop DeLuca was half-asleep and half-drunk when he stumbled off the National Express coach at Victoria Coach Station. His joints ached and the inside of his mouth was dry. A storm had ripped the sky open and rain poured down in sheets. Lightning flashed. Thunder rumbled. The only other passenger alighting with him was a sozzled Santa Claus who'd got on at York carrying a broken acoustic guitar without a case. He staggered off the coach and put up a black umbrella that flapped like bat's wings, he headed off in the direction of the nearest Kebab Shop

Be-Bop took in his surroundings. All around him, police sirens wailed and mobs of drunken youths staggered down the road toward the seemingly endless oasis of pubs, bars, nightclubs and kebab shops. A constellation of neon signs trailed down the road towards a Chinese takeaway that was adorned with Christmas lights, hi-energy music pounding from it, drowning out the sound of the boozed-up revellers that staggered in and out of its entrance. He turned up the collar on his overcoat, picked up his saxophone and stalked across the road toward a taxi rank. A lone, battered taxi cab was waiting like the last remaining whore in a run-down bordello. As Be-Bop approached the taxi, a behemoth barged past him, almost knocking him off his feet.

'I reckon that's for me, squire,' said a Shrek lookalike in a black leather jacket.

Be-Bop grabbed his arm but he brushed him aside without even bothering himself to look at him. Be-Bop put a hand on his shoulder. He froze. Be-Bop stepped in front of him.

'Excuse me, mate,' said Be-Bop. 'I think I was before you.'

Shrek stepped forward and glared at him, eyes like bullet holes.

'I'm not your mate, cunt,' he growled, and pushed Be-Bop backwards. He fell into a massive puddle.

Shrek wrenched open the taxi door and forced himself into the cramped cab's passenger seat. In seconds, the taxi pulled out with a squeal, splashing the tanned legs of a small group of scantily-clad teenage girls, who shrieked hysterically.

'What a cheeky fucker,' Be-Bop muttered, as he struggled to his feet. Wished he was younger. The joints not so stiff. The reactions not so slow.

He walked up to the taxi rank and waited in the rain listening to the monosyllabic yammering of a group of youths that had just puked up near him. There were no more taxis around and so, with Sisyphean resignation, he trudged towards the city centre. A familiar face beamed out from a large billboard beside St Martin's church, that loomed over the street. A dapper man in his sixties holding a foaming pint of bitter. At first he thought it was a beer advert then he realised it was a poster for a political party. The elections were coming up, it seemed. Not that Be-Bop cared a jot about politics. Though he did once have a Screaming Lord Sutch record.

A storm had gouged open the battered and bruised sky and he eventual took shelter from the downpour in Joe Fagan's Pub, a dingy basement bar just round the corner from Tottenham Court Road tube station. As he walked down the steps and into the bar, a sense of dread smothered him. He pushed his saxophone under an arm, took off his beret and shook the rain from it.

The cramped bar was barely lit by buzzing, dim red light bulbs. The walls were cluttered with the fading covers of old rockabilly LPs. A Wurlitzer jukebox played The Rumblers' *Boss* and Be-Bop noticed that the bar only had San Miguel and Estrella on draft. A small group of soaked Japanese tourists dressed as Sherlock Holmes sat huddled around the bar's lone table sipping bottles of Guinness and sneezing. God, Be-Bop hated London. It was a parasitic city. Nothing original ever came from the shithole. It was all stolen culture that had been watered down for the soft southern tossers. Still, at least you could get a drink here on New Year's Day. That wasn't such an easy task back up north.

He leaned on the bar and inhaled the twinkling bottles of spirits.

'What'll it be, sunshine?' said the barman, a handsome old Irishman with a bad ginger wig.

Be-Bop looked at the clock. Too early for the good stuff, he supposed.

'A pint of Estrella should do the trick,' he said.

Spanish beer was as weak as piss and normally he wouldn't touch the stuff but since he needed to keep his head out of the shed for a little bit longer it was just what the doctor ordered. Well, the doctor had actually ordered him to stay off the booze completely but there was no way he could survive a trip to London completely sober.

The Japanese tourists got up and left and Be-Bop put his beer on the table and sat down. Sighed. He put his saxophone case on the table.

The bar had the smell of a soggy nun, and a dead one at that. It was probably what the soft southern ponces called character. It had been a little less than a year since he'd last been down to the big smoke. At the time, he had delivered a payment from his boss, Captain Cutlass, to Mad Tony Cook. Payment for getting rid of Half-Pint Harry Hebb, if only by accident. This time the dosh was going in the other direction, though. He was there to collect. And do a bit of work for the Cooks.

Be-Bop sniffed loudly and the barman seemed to twig on and lit an incense stick which didn't particularly seem to help a great deal. He looked at Be-Bop, shrugged and made a half-hearted attempt at restocking the fridge with bottles of Sol.

Be-Bop took out an old copy of the Sunday Times and started on the crossword. Did about three quarters of it in ten minutes but he couldn't concentrate and asked the barman to switch on the TV. He always felt like a fish out of water when he was south of Seatown. A day trip to Middlesbrough was a mini trauma these days.

'There y'go,' said the barman, handing him the remote control.

The Discovery Channel was showing a programme about killer ants and Be-Bop quickly switched over. He hated insects almost as much as he hated London. In fact, he hated nature in general and watching the Discovery Channel always made him feel uncomfortable, itchy.

He scratched himself and channel surfed until he settled on a 24-hour news channel that was showing a report on a fun fair in Brighton that had been attacked by terrorists earlier that day. Apparently, there had been a bomb in the ghost train and another in the Ferris wheel. The number of dead and injured seem to escalate as he watched the program, and the barman quickly turned over to a game show.

'Always nice to see Brucie on the box,' said Marty Cook, as he shuffled down the stairs, shaking a massive pink golfing umbrella. He was wearing a black Hugo Boss suit and bespoke black overcoat.

He held out a hand and Be-Bop shook it.

'Nice to see you, to see you nice,' said Marty.

'Same to you,' said Be-Bop. 'I've never liked the bloke myself, though. I was always more of a Bob Monkhouse man.'

'What you drinking?' said Marty.

'I'll have another pint of this soppy Spanish slop,' said Be-Bop. He cringed inwardly as he remembered that Marty's wife was Spanish though the quip didn't seem to bother Marty.

The barman served Marty and switched off the television. Marty sat down as Billie Holliday sang about violets and furs.

'How's tricks, Marty?' said Be-Bop. He downed the remainder of his first pint and moved the new one closer.

'Not too bad, not too good,' said Marty. 'Things are a little stagnant at the moment to be honest. You?'

'Aw, pretty much the same as you. Cutlass is practically legit now and boring with it. He's buying up every club and wine bar in the town and giving them American themed names: 42nd Street, 5th Avenue and the like. He's even bought a fleet of New York style yellow cabs.'

Marty chuckled. 'If you can make it there, you can make it anywhere.'

'I know. But it seems to be working out okay for him. I make more money playing gigs these days than working for Cutlass, truth be told. I've got a couple of jobs while I'm down here, including a gig or two for your Uncle Tony. Should make up the shortfall. How's your brother?'

'Father Tim or the other one?'

'Aw, I meant Tim. The proper one. I keep forgetting about Richard Sanderson. How do you get along with him, anyway?'

Be-Bop's last visit to London had coincided with the Cook brothers discovering that they had a half-brother that they hadn't known about.

'I don't have that much contact with him, thankfully,' said Marty. 'He seems to be a bit of a knob end. He turns up at La Salsa every now and then, out of his face on Colombian marching powder. Usually makes a bit of a tit of himself. Still, he's my half-brother so I've got to keep him half-sweet just to keep dad happy.'

'Your dad still in the nick?'

The barman came over and started clearing the table next to them. They both gave him the 1000-yard stare.

'A little privacy, please,' said Marty.

The barman flushed.

'Yeah, er, sure, no probs.'

He put a few empty glasses on a tray and took them back to the bar.

'And turn up the music, eh?' said Be-Bop.

Joni Mitchell's *Coyote* was turned up accordingly.

Be-Bop turned back to Marty.

'So, you were saying about your dad,' he said.

'Yeah, he's still inside. He was due a shot at probation but the daft arse only went and dropped a tab of acid into a warden's tea and the bloke went loopy, pretending to be Zorro.'

'Sounds like a laugh.'

'Yeah, but it put the kibosh on dad's early release.'

'How did they find out it was your dad that spiked the drink?'

'Someone grassed him up, would you believe.'

'Really? That wasn't a particularly clever move was it?'

'Not a lot. Apparently, the grass in question, Marko Hammonds, has since converted to Islam in the hope that the Muslim Nation will protect him from dad.'

'And how's that working out?'

'Not so good. The swastika tattoo on Hammonds' forehead may be hindering things a tad, mind you.'

'So, are Tim and your Uncle Tony doing okay?'

'Tim's doing some cleaning work for Uncle Tony at the moment so I've not seen much of him. Might meet up with him later today. And as for Tony, well … let's just say he's been having a few relapses. He's re-earning his nick name.'

'The voices?'

Marty nodded.

'And visions,' said Marty. 'The whole of the family visit him regularly. Well, the dead ones. He keeps dressing up in his old army gear and listening to Glen Miller. Quoting The Goons. Having flashbacks and the like.'

He stared into space for a moment and then shoved a hand into his coat pocket.

'Anyway, before I forget …'

He passed a brown envelope over to Be-Bop.

'Cheers,' said Be-Bop. 'How's Squeaky working out anyway?'

'Like you said before, the geezer's no brain surgeon but he does what you tell him and seems to have his ear to the ground. When his nose isn't in the coke.'

'Yeah, he's pretty reliable but don't ask him to do anything to complicated. I'm surprised you need more foot soldiers though.'

'Yeah, well, local London criminals aren't what they used to be. Got ideas above their station.'

'Well, that's not Squeaky for sure.'

Marty's phone vibrated in his pocket. He took it out.

'Speak of the devil,' he said.

He listened for a moment and smiled.

'Of course do it. If you see a window of opportunity, Squeaky,' said Marty 'Then jump right in. Head-first if you have to.'

He listened again.

'No, I don't want you to smash the bloody window. Those trucks are worth a fortune and cost an arm and a leg to fix. Just nick the bleedin' thing.'

He rolled his eyes.

Be-Bop looked away, pretended to do the crossword.

'Things might just be looking up,' said Marty.

***

A chilly, rainy and windswept New Year's Day morning in a grimy North London pub car park wasn't normally what DI Niki Scrace would consider a cause for great jollity and mirth but, despite the combined nips of her hangover and the bitter cold, she couldn't help sniggering.

'Now, that's not something you see every day is it?' said DS Ronnie Burke, dragging his massive square head out of the boot of a rusty, old red Audi and smirking. He ran a hand through his long blond hair.

'Not a lot, Ronnie,' said Scrace. 'Not a lot.'

She sighed as he fastened her black raincoat tight around her muscular frame and tied back her red hair. She took out some chap stick and ran it across her lips, gagged a little, and cursed herself for going to the pub on a work night. Especially with the low tolerance for booze that she had these days, ever since the operation. Mind you, it was New Year's Eve and she wasn't to know that she'd be hauled out of her pit at the crack of dawn to attend the scene of a truck hijacking.

Ronnie had knocked back enough Stella Artois to sink a ship when they'd been in the pub the night before but he looked as right as rain as he bent down to look closer at the unconscious body in the car boot. Well, no rougher than he usually looked, anyway. He took hold of the little fat man by the cheek and gave him a little slap. No reaction. Tried again and the fat man grunted and started to snore like a Kalashnikov.

'Well, at least he's alive,' said Ronnie.

He sniffed and gagged.

'Jeez! It smells like they used enough chloroform on him to knock out an elephant. He'll have a hell of a hangover when he wakes up.'

Ronnie stepped away from the car and stretched, yawned.

'I just hope for him that the marker pen's not permanent but I suspect it is,' said Scrace.

She leaned over and used a sleeve of her raincoat to try to wipe off the Spiderman mask that had been drawn on the truck driver's face, and noticed Ronnie looking at her arse.

'No luck,' she said.

'I wasn't looking,' said Ronnie, who then grinned at his guilty mistake.

'That would be a "doh" moment, I think,' said Scrace.

'Aye,' said Ronnie. 'Soz.'

A sharp gust of wind blew a rattling beer can between them.

'A tumbleweed moment,' said Ronnie.

He stuffed a hand into his raincoat pocket, pulled out a packet of orange Tic Tacs and offered them to Scrace, who shook her head, still glaring at him. He opened his mouth wide and poured a mouthful in. Started crunching loudly.

Scrace watched a pair of grubby seagulls attack each other mid-air and wondered how they'd found their way from the sea to Finchley. She'd often wondered how she'd ended up here. It had been a long and painfully winding road from Whitby to London, and she wasn't particularly enamoured of the place, to be sure. Still, needs must.

She looked over at The Wenlock Arms, wondering if it was open for a bit of shelter and a hot cuppa.

'It's supposed to be a decent boozer that,' said Ronnie, he nodded toward the pub. 'But it doesn't open till the evening.'

'Really?' said Scrace. She looked around at the wasteland surrounding the pub. Shattered glass, discarded condoms and beer cans. The building itself looked pretty nice from the outside but she'd imagined it being a dump once you stepped inside. 'It actually has customers?'

'Yeah, it's very big on the real ale circuit apparently,' he said.

'Alright, if you like that kind of thing, I suppose. I prefer a bottle of Kopparberg myself.'

'I'm not that fond of that real ale cobblers, either,' said Ronnie. 'Smells like IBS.'

Scrace laughed.

'And the drinkers are even worse,' said Ronnie. 'Hairy dandruffy types. They're a stranger to deodorant. Whenever I'm in a real ale pub, I keep expecting Operation Yewtree to burst in.'

'Now then, now then,' said Scrace.

They both chuckled.

'What was the truck carrying anyway?' said Scrace.

'Comics, apparently,' said Ronnie, between crunches.

'Comics? The Beano and The Dandy?'

'Naw, American ones, Batman, Spiderman and the like.'

'Hence the comedy face-painting,' said Scrace.

'I suppose so. They reckon it's a massive collection, owned by none other than Matt Cane. Heard of him?'

'That American film star that's just moved into that horrific mock-castle thing up the road?'

'That's the geezer. Ever seen any of his films?' said Ronnie. He pushed the Tic Tacs back into his pocket.

'Unfortunately so. He's certainly no Larry Olivier but he's dead good at running, mind you, I'll give him that,' said Scrace.

'Well, he might not be much cop at the acting lark but he's worth a bob or two and so is his comic collection.'

'Funny old world,' said Scrace.

'You're telling me,' said Ronnie. 'Nowt as queer as folk, as they say on Coronation Street.'

He winked and grinned weakly. Scrace scowled at him again and he flushed.

'Yeah, no, but listen, I was just …you know …' His words petered out.

'Take a chill pill Phil,' said Scrace.

She suddenly felt smothered by the cold and stamped her feet. Along with everything else, her circulation was shit these days, too. She nodded toward a small brown van that was parked in front of a closed down cinema on the other side of the street. The phrase 'HOTSNAX' was emblazoned on the side of the van in Day-Glo colours.

'Fancy a coffee while the boffins do their stuff?' she said.

'Indeed,' said Ronnie. 'A particularly tickety-boo idea, that.'

They walked towards the van as a SOCO started examining the red Audi and a couple of policemen lifted the snoozing truck driver from the boot.

A grubby white transit van pulled up outside the snack van and a group of Goth's stumbled out. Ronnie shook his head in disgust.

'Look at the state of that. Could do with a good tubbing and spell in the army, the lot of them. Freaks and weirdoes everywhere you look these days.'

He glanced at Scrace.

'I mean, you know …'

Scrace grinned.

'You've got a case of foot in mouth disease today, Ronnie,' she said.

'Aye, I am making a bit of a tit-end of myself.'

'So, go on then ask,' said Scrace.

'Ask what?'

'Whatever you want. If you ask me I'll tell you.'

'Well …'

The small group of shivering Goths stood in front of the snack van smoking pin sized roll ups. Scrace could smell the tempting aroma of ganja. She walked up to them, showed her ID card and they shuffled out of the way.

'What can I do you for, Inspector?' said the man behind the counter, an ageing skinhead with a faded swastika tattoo on his forehead and a tattooed tear below his left eye. He looked vaguely familiar to Scrace but there were plenty of that type around.

'A couple of coffees, please,' she said.

'Black or white?' said the skinhead.

'Black, like my women,' said Scrace. She winked.

The skinhead grimaced.

'Make sure you get a receipt for expenses, Chief,' said Ronnie.

Scrace nodded. Anything they bought from this joint would easily come into the ever dwindling expenses budget, she was sure. The van itself wasn't exactly first class, the owner obviously only on nodding terms with concepts like hygiene and cleanliness. The skinhead enthusiastically sang along to a Tina Turner song that leaked from the radio. If this was the best, well, the country was in an even worse state than she thought.

'Go on then,' said Scrace. She collected the coffee and handed one to Ronnie. They walked slowly back toward the crime scene. 'Ask. You won't be the first.'

'Alright.' said Ronnie. He slurped the coffee. Burnt his lip.

'Tit wank!'

Scrace laughed.

'That'll be that Karma, I reckon,' she said.

Ronnie looked at Scrace.

'Did it hurt? The op?' he said.

'Well would it hurt you to have your cock cut off and your bollocks rammed inside you?'

Ronnie grimaced.

'I hope I never have to find out,' he said.

'Well, look at my arse like that again and you'll find out sharpish, alright?'

***

Madge's Mini Coffee Pot was super-hot and jam packed with people dressed as The Muppets. What looked like a bunch of musicians in beer stained fancy dress costumes nursed their hangovers and whispered to each other in croaky voices. Behind the counter, Madge, a midget with a withered arm, was serving tea in half pint glasses to Fozzie Bear and Gonzo, both of whom had the heads from their costumes under their arms and were sweating like pigs. A sound system that was twice as large as Madge herself blasted out a U2 song from a pair of raspy speakers.

'All is far from bleedin' quiet this New Year's Day,' said Father Tim to Miss Piggy. She chuckled, burped and put her head in her arms. Knocked her guitar over.

'Kermit, you tosser,' she said to herself, in a Welsh accent. 'You just don't know, don't know, you just …'

Kermit was sat at another table, sleeping. Using his head for a pillow.

Tim watched the streamers of steam rise from his mug of strong, sweet tea. Madge brought over a full English breakfast with extra chips and placed the plate in front of him.

'Get stuck in to that little lot Father T,' said Madge.

'Don't mind if I do!' said Tim, snowing salt over his chips. He smothered it with brown sauce and vinegar before tucking in.

Satisfied with his first few bites, he glanced out of the steamed up window as his brother Marty got out of a black cab and walked across the road, holding a bright golfing umbrella that flapped in the wind like a bird trying to escape. Always the dapper Dan man.

Marty walked into the café looking well pissed off. He spotted Tim and grunted.

'Flashbacks to Nam,' said Marty as he sat down.

'That'd be Chelt-nam, would it?' said Tim. 'Had a flutter on the Gold Cup?'

'Sharp, that. As a cutthroat razor. No, it was a year ago that we met up here to try and sort out the mess up with Uncle Tony's briefcase. Remember?'

'Oh, yes I remember it well. You wore exactly the same clobber then. A tad overdressed, for the environment, I think.'

'So says a man wearing a cravat, albeit a bloodstained cravat. Anyway, I didn't know you paid such close attention to my sartorial carryings on,' said Marty. 'Nice to know that the effort I make isn't wasted.'

'Consistency is the city hobgoblin of little minds,' said Tim, he took off the cravat and stuffed it in his pocket. Rubbed the scar around his throat.

'If you like, bro,' said Marty. 'I'm partial to a hobnob myself. What's the score with you, anyway?'

'Just cleaning up for Uncle Tony. Tidying up bits and bobs.'

'Bits and bobs by the name of Aldo Calvino and Ron Moody?' said Marty.

He picked up a napkin and shined his yin and yang cufflinks.

'Indeed. And a few other waifs and strays along the way,' said Tim.

'That bleedin' briefcase. It's been more bloody effort than it's worth.'

'Indeed. You got anything on, business wise?'

'As a matter of fact, I do. A nice little earner, if all goes well.' Marty looked at his Rolex. 'Yep, some very tasty valuables should be heading my way any moment now, with a little help from one of our northern friends.'

'Tell me more. What is it? Diamonds? Bonds?'

'Comics, actually?'

'Comics?'

'Yep, American ones. Mainly Marvel. Early Spiderman, including the number one, and all in mint condition.'

'Tidy! Wouldn't mind a few of them myself though, as you know, I've always been more of a DC man.'

'Me too, though The Dark Shite Rises put paid to that.'

'Yeah. Man of Steel was even worse. More depressing than this weather,' said Tim.

He drained his tea and looked out of the window. Rain still poured.

'Not exactly Cool Britannia is it?' said Tim.

Marty followed Tim's gaze out of the window. The rain battered the glass. A Tizer can skittered down the street. A fat Santa Clause stood in front of *Booze n News,* drinking a can of Special Brew, scratching his buttocks.

'Not a lot.'

'Are you still thinking of pissing off to Spain for good?' said Tim.

'On stinky, rainy, windy days like this, it really doesn't seem too bad an idea, to be honest,' said Marty.

A drunk in a shiny suit staggered up and vomited against a charity shop's metal shutters.

'You can't buy class, eh?' said Marty.

Tim took a pair of half-moon glasses from his top pocket. Put them on.

'I think I know him. Isn't that Paul Garner?' said Tim

'Could be,' said Marty, squinting. 'Looking a bit more respectable since his Goth days, if it is him.'

'I remember that his mum Tina was so chuffed when her blue eyed boy got into Sunderland Poly. They had a big knees-up for him in The Blue Anchor. Dave Prowse tuned up in his Green Cross Code Man uniform and did a striptease.'

'Knowing Dave he probably got hammered and started prattling on about *Star Wars*. How he was the true Darth Vader. Ended up in tears.'

'Of course,' said Tim. 'A creature of narrow habit, our Dave.'

'What did he study?' said Marty.

'Dave Prowse? The Green Cross Code was as far as it got, I think. Maybe bicycle proficiency.'

'No, you plonker, Paul Garner.'

'Ah. Communication studies, if I remember correctly.'

'Quite apt since he's now working at the car phone warehouse.'

'From little acorns, a mighty oak grows,' said Tim.

Garner wiped his mouth and wandered over to the Santa Clause. Gave him a handful of coins. Santa fished in his sack and pulled out a can of beer. Gave it to Garner who opened it up and knocked it back.

'Out with the old, in with the new,' said Father Tim.

***

There was a violent storm brewing inside Matt Cane's perfectly coiffured skull. A Tsunami. A hurricane. A volcanic eruption to pale the one that decimated Pompeii. The actor was on the verge of having one of his infamous temper tantrums – pretty much identical to the one that had been posted all over the internet when he was working on the last Christopher Nolan film *Conundrum*. The fit of temper that had earned him the industry nickname 'Cane In The Ass.'

The cause for that particular explosion had been when one of the cleaners had messed with the Feng Shui in his trailer. Cane quite naturally blamed the cleaner for him screwing up his lines during a particularly stressful scene with Leo and Gwyneth. And he let the third-world bitch know it in no uncertain terms, that was for sure.

Of course, Cane wasn't to know that the cleaner would use her Smartphone to record the outburst and post it on You Tube, was he? How much did these people get paid to be able to afford smart phones, anyway? He was even more pissed because he only found out about his meltdown going viral when his ex-wife's most recent husband phoned to congratulate him on the performance. The donation to the Inuit Preservation Fund, or whatever it was called, had hurt too. But this morning's phone call had really skewered his heart. Some limey bastard had stolen his hallowed comic book collection.

'This is just not goddamn acceptable,' he yelled and slammed down the receiver on gold-plated phone. It clattered down the side of his four poster bed. He closed his eyes to control his breathing.

'I cannot believe this,' he muttered to himself.

Cane had nurtured that comic book collection since he was a kid. Whenever a first issue of a new comic was published he'd always bought three copies; one to read, one to seal in an air proof plastic bag, and one to be signed by the artists and writers when he tracked them down at comic conventions. Or at their homes.

He couldn't believe that the cherished collection had been stolen. The financial loss was bad enough but the spiritual cost was deeper. Those comics had given him life lessons. Taught him how you had to be strong to survive. When his dad had absconded, Frank Miller had been like a surrogate father to him – *The Dark Knight Returns* was Cane's bible. His life manual.

He got off the bed and took off his silk pyjamas. Checked his muscular body in the mirror and was pleased with what he saw. Felt a little better as he stroked his stomach. He tied back his long black hair and went over to the yoga mat. It had been carefully placed in front of a massive bay window that looked out across a finely trimmed lawn surrounded by bizarrely sculpted topiary. Still fuming, he assumed the Lotus Position.

He tried to focus. To let his anger slip away but the red mist consumed him.

'Om! Om! Goddamn Om!' he shouted.

He banged his fists on the floor and massaged his forehead for a few minutes. Then banged his fists the floor again.

He could see the relaxation techniques were getting nowhere. Why the hell had he come to Jolly Old England anyway? The place was about as jolly as carpet burns. Rain. Wind. Rain. Wind. The weather was particularly sucky. Especially in fall, or whatever the hell they called it here. That was another thing he hated. The way they talked. They didn't even understand real English here, even though they would all be speaking German if it wasn't for the good old US of A saving their asses, but they conveniently seemed to forget that. Ungrateful bastards.

He reached over and picked up the gold plated phone, dialled furiously.

'Rossiter,' he said after a moment. 'Someone has fucked up big time. And I want their balls on a plate … no not for breakfast you creepy Limey asshole! Get me Harvey. That dumb hick shyster needs to get her tight ass over here and Napalm this joint.'

He slammed the phone onto the floor, got back into the lotus position and farted noisily. And it smelled like victory.

Marty Cook let out a silent fart as he lay back in his black-leather armchair and swigged his mug of sweet tea. He was feeling smug. Super bleedin' smug. Maybe things were looking up for him, at last. If you listened to the blah-blah-blah on the telly or in the papers, the import and export trade wasn't what it used to be but then that just depended on what you imported or exported, didn't it? And Marty had his nob stuck in the bunghole of more than a few well-tasty niche markets, that was for sure.

He straightened the trousers of his suit as he stood up and stretched. Glanced in the mirror to check that his famous blond curls still had that carefully windswept look. Felt pretty damned good, for a change.

He checked his smartphone, and sent a couple of text messages to make sure the buyer was still interested in the stuff that Squeaky Thompson had managed to purloin that morning. Not that the comics would be difficult to shift elsewhere, if it all went pear-shaped, but discretion was a key part of his business. And this particular client was as kosher as they came. Well, as kosher as lawyers came. At first Marty had only been interested in the truck that Squeaky had pinched but when he'd realised how valuable the contents were, his focus changed.

Marty's phone bleeped and he read the confirmation. Smirked as he saw that an international bank transfer had dolloped a massive wad of dosh into his account. What a bloody good start to the day.

He swivelled the armchair and looked around his office. It wasn't exactly the most prepossessing of places. It was definitely in need of more than a lick of paint, he hadn't redecorated it for donkey's years. His elation slowly slipped away and he felt a weight on his chest as he thought about how he and Veronica could be having the time of their life in Andalucía, no doubt about it. And there he was stuck in Acton, the claggy armpit of West London. An area that seemed to be getting more and more depressing the more gentrified it tried to be. He knew they should never have moved out of Essex but Veronica had said there were too many foreigners moving in and lowering the tone of the place.

He picked up his Crombie and headed out of the office. When he walked into the warehouse, he could see that most of the boxes had already been unpacked. He sniffed. There was an acrid smell in the air. The sour smell of success.

'Now, be careful with this little lot, lads,' he said, his voice like broken glass. 'Precious and valuable cargo, the lot of it.'

'Who'd have thunk it,' said Squeaky Thompson, a massive Michelin Man with a helium-balloon voice. 'People paying a fortune for a bunch of grubby old kids' funny books.'

'One man's grubby comic is another man's fine art,' said Marty. 'Maybe that's why they call it filthy lucre.'

Thompson squeaked a laugh and started to sing the theme from *Different Strokes* with a massive shit-eating-grin sliding across his face.

'Oi, and make sure you completely barbecue the truck. Don't try selling it off to any of your tight-arsed Northern mates, alright, Squeaky?' said Marty.

'Okey dokey, boss.'

Marty held Squeaky's gaze for a moment just to make sure he'd gotten the message. Squeaky was a relatively new recruit to Marty's firm and although he was more than enthusiastic he wasn't the sharpest knife in the toaster. But then he was a Geordie and they weren't exactly renowned for their massive intellect. Or dress sense, by the looks of Squeaky, who seemed to dress exclusively in Primark cast offs that were at least a size too small.

As Marty headed out of the door, he plucked his phone from his pocket with a clammy hand. This was going to be a corker of a day; he could feel it in his waters.

***

This was becoming the shittiest day of Kenny Rogan's life. He'd woken up in his truck's cabin at the crack of dawn and staggered out into the cold to have a gypsy's kiss in a pub car park. While he was having a slash, some twat had stuck a hanky of chloroform in his mush and he'd woken up the back of a shitty red Astra with a bunch of coppers laughing at him, his truck well gone.

He'd felt as if he'd had the worst hangover of his life as those two detectives had interrogated him. Harangued him, more like it. The ginger bint had been alright, mind you, she'd been the 'good cop' of the duo he supposed. But the bloke with the raggy tash had been a right pain. Kept bursting out laughing. Going on about lorry driving being a 'great responsibility' for some reason.

And then Kenny had found out he'd had a Spiderman mask drawn on his face. It had taken him all morning to scrub that shit off. Bleedin' hurt it had, too. His face was red raw now and he'd coated it with aftershave balm, which stunk.

The truck itself was an Actros Titan, worth over a million, and the cargo – a load of old American comics – was worth even more than that. Some daft yank actor had paid him a fortune to deliver it safely and now look what had happened. So much for going legit. He'd ended up so far up shit creek an outdoor motor wouldn't have helped never mind a paddle.

He'd collapsed into bed when he'd eventually got home but he'd had yet another attack of cramp and almost fell out of bed. And, as per usual, he couldn't get back to sleep once he'd woken up. And now his missus wouldn't even let him have a pork pie to calm his nerves.

'Just a mini one,' he whined. 'It's for the stress.'

He scratched his flaky scalp. His eczema had been getting worse over the last few months and the lads in The Blue Anchor had started winding him up about it, calling him Mr Cornflakes and The Minging Defective.

'Those are for the kids and anyway you know what Dr Gupta told you about eating fatty food,' she said. 'Your cholesterol level is higher than Big Ben.'

Sandra slammed the fridge door shut, almost trapping Kenny's pudgy fingers.

'Now I'm going to cook my breakfast. I've got to work a double shift today. We'll be needing the money,' she said.

Sandra Rogan was a good six inches shorter than Kenny but it was usually the look in her dark eyes that did all the violence she needed. She stood with her hands on hips, glaring at him and looking well-fit in her nurse's uniform.

'But it wasn't my fault. I only …'

'Out!'

Kenny shuffled into the massive, pristine living room and switched on the TV. His heart sank further when he saw *The Jeremy Kyle Show*; a bunch of unemployable nightmares with mangled teeth were whinging about how hard their life was. The nation's underachievers. Scabs on the bollocks of society. Kenny despised them, he really did. Bringing back National Service would do the lot of them the world of good. Did him no harm.

He flicked through the channels but couldn't find anything to hold his attention. There was another remote control that he could have used to see what was on the digital channels but he'd never got the hang of using that and didn't want to ask Sandra.

He was well and truly pissed off and decided there and then that if he ever saw the twats that had taken his truck he would friggin' well make them pay. He sighed as he sank deeper into his favourite armchair. The straight life really wasn't all it was cracked up to be.

'Oh, and Kenny,' shouted Sandra over the sound of frying bacon.

His stomach churned and a shudder went through him.

'Yes, my little bowl of muesli,' he said.

'Marty Cook rang to say he has a job for you tomorrow night at the club, if you want.'

'I told him loads of times before that I don't do THAT anymore. I'm a respectable businessman now.'

'Well, it's up to you. I just passed the message on. But, you know it's our Kelsey's Holy Communion next month and you promised …'

Kenny let the sound of Sandra's voice fade out and tried in vain to use one of the millions of remote controls they seemed to have to turn the television over.

He was tired of being in the shadow of the Cook family, he really was. Last year's shenanigans recovering a lost briefcase for Mad Tony Cook had taken the biscuit, even though Kenny had been the one who'd lost it. He'd worked for the Cook's for donkey's years and had been well chuffed to go it on his own. Then, thinking of the stolen truck, and the dosh he'd lost out on, he thought, why not? Marty was the most tolerable of the Cooks and had always treated him right. With a bit of luck, he might even have time to sneak in a sneaky sausage roll on the way there.

STOOL PIGEON

'If you gaze into the abyss' said Marty, with a lop-sided smirk. 'The abyss also gazes … and sometimes winks at you and blows you a kiss.'

He kissed the dart in his hand. Winked at the dartboard.

'Very profound, that,' said Be-Bop DeLuca, who was leaning against the bar drinking a pint of orange and water, feeling old. Weary. His guts were really playing him up and he needed to keep off the drink for a while, which didn't please him a great deal. His beret and saxophone case were on the bar beside him.

Marty threw the dart at the dartboard with a dramatic flourish but great force. It hit the bull's eye dead centre, as he knew it would.

'Shoot that poison arrow to my arse!' he said.

'That's the sign of a misspent youth that is,' said Be-Bop. 'Too much time in the pub.'

'Did me alright, sunshine,' said Tim. 'Those afternoons with Keef and Ronnie in The Cricketers, over Richmond, opened more than a few doors for me, too.'

He held out a hand and waggled his fingers. Be-Bop took out his wallet and plucked out a tenner. Handed it to Marty.

'Haven't you got better things to do with your time than hanging around deserted pubs?' said Be-Bop.

Marty sat on a bar stool. Finished his pint of Carling. Burped. Held up a finger.

'Listen to that,' he said.

The Essex Arms was almost empty. A wiry old duffer sat nursing a half-pint of Guinness and reading a battered copy of Ivanhoe, pausing occasionally to sniff the pages. A tall Goth sat near the door playing with his smartphone, a full pint of cider and black on his table.

'Listen to what? I can't hear a thing,' said Be-Bop. 'Except Mr Snifter over there.'

'I know. That's just it. That's the good bit. Silence. There's no piped music played here. No jukebox. No fruit machines. No telly. No radio. Nothing. It's an oasis. Nothing to distract you from yourself.'

'No yuppies yammering on, too. They're everywhere down here. Everywhere has been gentrified by the looks of it.'

'That's an added bonus, mate. Over the years I've come to appreciate the value of silence.'

Be-Bop fiddled with his hearing aid.

'I know what you mean,' he said. 'It's a rare commodity these days. It's not just the music, though. Over the years, I've heard so much stuff, good and bad that I can tune it out. Pedestrian pub rock bands and dreary acoustic troubadours. There's a gadgy plays the circuit round my way and calls himself The Man Who Would Be Sting. Bloody torture, he is. Yeah, that's bad enough but it's all them bleeps and bloops and shit from the one armed bandits and the like that do my napper in. They're everywhere. I even went to the library the other day and it was full of all that interactive cobblers.'

'Sign of the times, mate.'

'Well, we're certainly alright here,' said Be-Bop. 'This place is like a morgue. Mind, you'd think the owners might want to do something to jazz it up, like.'

'Naw, they don't, mate. I don't, to be more precise.'

Be-Bop grinned. Marty hadn't seen that happen before and it was a tad unsettling.

'This is your place? Nice one,' said Be-Bop. He took out one of his electronic cigarettes. 'Does it make its dosh back?'

Marty got off the bar stool and went around the bar. Poured himself another pint of lager.

'Pays for itself and a bit more. The lunch sessions do well alright, what with that advertising agency nearby. And that IT firm. Pub grub is where it's at these days.'

'The phrase pub lunch sends a shiver through my spine,' said Be-Bop. 'The once lovely and sedate local pub is now cluttered with pasty-faced secretaries ordering coffee. Eating sun-dried tomatoes. Some things are beneath contempt but I still contempt them.'

'Things change,' said Marty. 'Times change. People change. Anyway, want another? A proper drink?'

'Naw,' said Be-Bop. 'I've got three wheels on my wagon. I'll keep rolling along for a bit longer, like.'

'Let's get down to business, then.'

He sat next to Be-Bop.

'Know anything about this stuff?'

He took out his smartphone. Showed a picture to Be-Bop.

Be-Bop squinted.

'Now, that is ... a hell of a lot of comics. They worth something?' he said.

'Looks it.'

'Where did you get 'em?'

'Squeaky Thompson, would you believe. That was what he phoned me about yesterday. He tea-leafed them from some pub car park over Finchley way. Got some swanky truck, too, though it looks like we'll have to torch that.'

'Right place, right time, eh?'

'Exactly. I was thinking of getting Ron Moody to have a butcher's at it but it looks like he's gone AWOL,' said Marty.

'What about Aldo? You know the fat gadgy that's shacked up with that Albino bint.'

'Him too. Lost without a clue. Seems like the best fences in the city have gone walkabout.'

'What about some of your more legitimate contacts? The showbiz kids? The Stones? Jim Davidson? Rod The Mod? Max Clifford?'

'Naw, they're all squeaky clean these days. If this is the real deal then they'll keep well away from it. Anyway, Rod wouldn't put his hand in his pocket for anything. You know how tight he is. Remember that gig in Kentish Town?'

'Painfully well,' said Be-Bop. He stroked a scar on his temple.

'Right, then.'

Be-Bop finished his drink and put his beret on.

'I'll have a sniff around. I did hear about an American film star who's into all that sort of pop culture stuff and probably wouldn't mind it being a bit dodgy,' he said.

'Fair dos. The usual percent suit you?'

'Aye, that'll do nicely. Best be off. Got a bit of work on.'

Be-Bop picked up his saxophone.

'You got a gig?' said Marty.

'Aye, over Camden. The Jazz Café. Free Form Friday.'

'Thought you hated all that squeaky cobblers?'

'Not too keen but since the tinnitus it's pretty much all I can play. Anyway, it's easy enough to fake avant-garde jazz. Then I'm heading off to see your Uncle Tony. See what he has lined up for me.'

'Give me a ring when you find something out about the comics, then?'

'Will do,' said Be-Bop.

Marty went back to the bar. Took a newspaper from the rack and saw that Mr Snifter had gone and the lanky Goth had fallen asleep in the corner.

'It ain't rock 'n roll but I like it,' he muttered to himself.

***

The winter night bit like a savage beast, and heavy rain ripped through the sombre evening sky as Father Tim Cook stalked down Waterloo Road towards a small, brightly-painted flower stall, his black umbrella flapping in the wind like crows' wings.

The stall's owner was a giant of a man with a face so red that it looked as if it was about to explode any minute. Gregor was a fearsome sight, to be sure. The many lines on his face were like a record of his life's trials and tribulations. He'd hitchhiked to England from Slovenia as a teenager and had made his way around the country surviving as best he could until he eventually became one of London's most feared enforcers; a ferocious mercenary who was employed by the most powerful villains in the city – the Kray Twins, the Richardson Gang, and other gangsters that were less well known but just as violent. And The Cook Gang, of course. There had even been rumours that he'd turned into some sort of vampire hunter for a time. Father Tim wouldn't have put it past him, either.

Gregor locked up his stall and stuffed the day's takings into a money belt. The evenings were usually busy for him, men from the nearby offices, filled with guilt and alcohol, bought flowers for their neglected wives and girlfriends.

Father Tim waited outside a steamed up kebab shop, the smell of sizzling animal flesh making him want to heave. A stray

Rottweiler stuck its muzzle into a rubbish bin that was overflowing with fast food debris. Tim gave it a kick in the ribs. It yelped and ran off down a side street.

Gregor looked up and grinned as he saw his old friend for the first time in months. They shook hands, spoke quietly in Slovene and then Gregor locked up his stall. They headed down The Cut, past the trendy shops, bars and restaurants that were full of people celebrating the end of the working week.

A group of drunken middle-aged men in Manchester United football shirts staggered out of a Thai restaurant shouting racial abuse at an angry looking chef who was chasing them out and wielding a machete.

'Ah, Northern scum,' said Tim. 'Cultural ambassadors.'

'Indeed,' said Gregor, in the clipped RP English usually only found in 1940s public information films. 'Unfortunately, at certain times of year, they infest the streets of this great city like lice.'

One of the men – a short and stocky skinhead – staggered into Gregor who pushed him away disinterestedly. The other men laughed as he fell backwards into a puddle.

'You southern wankers,' said the skinhead as he struggled to get up, and slipped back down onto his arse.

'Yea, you old twats,' said a gangling long-haired Ginger with a stubbly beard. He balled his fists and lurched toward Gregor.

'Now maybe you need a bit of Northern hostility,' he said. 'I can …'

Before he could finish his sentence, Gregor kicked him in balls and Ginger collapsed onto the ground, whinging, tears in his eyes. Gregor pressed a foot onto the wailing man's knee.

The other men rushed toward Tim and Gregor.

'Southern twats!' shouted one of them.

Gregor grinned as he swiftly head-butted him. The thug's nose burst open and he screamed like a slaughtered pig. A couple of the others rushed towards Tim. Father Tim slammed one of them in the Adams apple with his fist and then kicked him in the groin. He stabbed another in the eye with his umbrella. Gregor head-butted another. Tim and Gregor punched and kicked, grinning as they did. In a matter of minutes, the thugs were in a pile on the ground, aching, groaning, moaning. Cursing.

Father Tim looked down at them with disgust.

'The standard of football hooligan is well below par these days, Gregor,' he said.

'Indeed,' said Gregor. 'All sound and fury signifying nothing. But you're mixing your sporting metaphors there.'

'Well, I'm gasping for a pint now, mind you,' said Tim, looking around for the nearest pub.

'Indeed. Indeed. I built up a bit of a thirst there myself.'

They stepped over the yobs and walked down a side street and into the first pub they saw. Ye Olde Stag was a faux traditional pub with far from traditional prices, as Father Tim noticed when he examined at the chalkboard behind the bar. The Best Of The Eagles leaked out of the sound system.

'A peaceful, easy feeling my arse,' said Tim. 'I can't stand The Eagles.'

'I'm rather fond of Don Henley myself,' said Gregor.

'Bleedin' pricey joint this is,' said Tim. 'I remember when this boozer was a real hole in the wall joint. All spit and sawdust.'

'The drinks are on the house,' said Kamilla the stern looking Polish barmaid, who had crossed herself when they walked in.

'As long as you're on your back I don't care where they are,' said Tim. He winked and the barmaid flushed.

'Sigmund Freud said that a blush is a supressed orgasm, did you know that Gregor?' said Tim.

'I did not, Father,' said Gregor. 'You are the font of all useless knowledge.'

'But I always thought that Freud was a bit of a fraud. Did you see what I did then?'

'I did, Father,' said Gregor. 'I did.'

The barmaid shuffled uncomfortably. Father Tim beamed a 1000-watt smile.

'Two pints of Nelson please, darling,' he said.

'Eh?' she said.

'Two pints of Stella,' said Tim. 'You know? Rhyming slang? Stella, as in Nelson Mandela?'

She shrugged and started pouring the lager.

'Bloody foreigners everywhere these days,' said Tim.

'You're telling me,' said Gregor.

They took their drinks over to a table in a darkened corner.

'So what's the story with your Uncle then? Is he starting some sort of Stalinist purge?' said Gregor.

'Not far off it,' said Tim, gulping his beer. 'And, accordingly, I have a little list, as Gilbert O Sullivan once said.'

Tim took out a betting slip with a list of names written on the back.

'And what have these poor unfortunate souls done?

'Ah well that goes back to the briefcase?'

'The silver briefcase?'

'Well, it was actually only stainless steel but yep that's the one. What do you know about it?'

'Only that your Uncle Tony hand been after an errant silver or stainless steel briefcase and its contents for a number of years and that a while back he actually managed to obtain it'

'Well, that's pretty much it but since then Uncle Tony has started to get a tad … mental. Paranoid. Like after Auntie Suzie died. He's worried that someone's going to TWOC his treasure. He's even locked it away in the house safe and that gaff has more security than Fort Knox. So, he's asked me to take care of any loose lips that might sink the ship.'

'There are some decent sorts on that list,' said Gregor

He tapped the betting slip.

'I mean, Ron Moody? He may look like a vampire … may actually be a vampire for all I know but …'

'I know, but what Uncle Tony wants …'

Suddenly, the doors to the pub burst open and the same bunch of drunken thugs that they'd encountered earlier staggered in, bringing a raging storm in with them.

'What a fucking shithole,' shouted the short, round skinhead that had fallen in the puddle.

'I hope it's cheap,' said the ginger one.

Kamilla, the barmaid came back from the toilets.

'It's got pussy, anyway,' said the skinhead; he grabbed Kamilla around the waist.

'Fancy a dance, pet,' he said, and dragged her around the room to the amusement of his mates.

Kamilla grinned and head-butted him. His nose burst open and he screamed like a slaughtered pig. She twirled away from him and bowed.

A couple of the other thugs rushed towards her but Gregor stepped out of the darkness and slammed one of them in the Adams apple with his fist and then kicked him in the groin. Father Tim head-butted another one of them. Gregor punched another in the guts and sent him sprawling into the bar. In a few minutes the thugs where in a heap on the floor of the pub.

'What a shower,' said Gregor.

'Pathetic, isn't it?' said Father Tim.

'Shall I call the police?' said Kamilla.

'I wouldn't bother. This lot are a bit of a waste of the constabularies' limited and stretched resources,' said Father Tim.

He bent down and picked up one of the thugs from the floor. Slapped his face.

'You won't be causing us any problems, will you?' he said.

He opened his jacket and tapped the gun in his shoulder holster. The wide eyed thug nodded.

'So, why not piss out of here before I start to get angry with you?' said Tim.

The yobs shuffled to their feet and out of the pub, whinging and groaning.

Tim turned to Kamilla, who was waving around a baseball bat.

'You won't be needing that love so could you put it down and put the telly on? It's nearly time for *The Antiques Roadshow.*

***

There were gnomes at the bottom of Niki Scrace's garden. Red ones, green ones, pink and striped ones. Gnomes that were dressed in traditional gnome garb and others that had been made up to look like policemen, cowboys, American Indians, sailors, soldiers, astronauts. Yes, she was the proud owner of the garden gnome version of the Village People. Not that she'd bought them herself, of course. They were there when she'd moved into the place.

One of the deals, when Ralphy Roberts – the owner of the 'compact terraced house' on Prestwick Road, Finchley that she called home – eventually deemed Scrace worthy enough to rent out to at 'a bargain price,' was that the gnomes would stay. And that Scrace would 'tend' them.

'What, you mean water them?' she'd said, in all innocence.

Ralphy, a long-retired star of stage, screen, pantomime and toilet roll advert voice-overs, had raised his black caterpillar eyebrows and boomed in an echoing Brian Blessed voice: 'If I was in the need of sarcasm young lady I should have picked up the telephone and spoken to one of my former wives!' and then he staggered off across the road to The Black Bull, which had just opened.

So, Scrace never did find out what he'd actually meant by 'tend', but one night after a spliff or two too many she'd hit upon the notion that he really meant for her to speak to them, and eventually she got into the habit of doing just that. Once a week, after she finished work, she sat there in the moonlight, smoking a joint and discussing her problems with the gnomes. She'd even developed favourites, Dixon the cop being, she assumed the best listener and Sitting Bull, the American Indian the wisest.

She wrapped her fake fur coat around her and pulled on her fingerless gloves. She stepped into the garden and sat on a white plastic chair. Took out her spliff and lit up. She inhaled and held it for a long time. Then she looked at the cowboy and nodded. Had a brief coughing fit. Took a sip from a bottle of water. Cleared her throat.

'Thanks for asking, Tex. It was so much better than last week, thanks,' she said. 'I didn't really expect them to accept me so easily. I mean, I'm sure there are more than a few jibes behind my back – I distinctly heard one bloke referring to me as 'The Ladyboy' and that Aerosmith song *Dude Looks Like A Lady* keeps mysteriously cropping up in the canteen when I go there – but it's what I'd expect from coppers. It's what we do. We wind each other up. 'Bust each other's chops', as you say in the States. Anyway, I've got skin like a rhino.'

She finished the joint and put it back in her old Rizla tin. Squinted at the traffic cop.

'Ronnie? He's fine, thanks. Tolerable, at least. He's been on about a million 'Coping with Diversity' courses lately and it seems to have help curb some of his less appropriate behaviour.'

The cowboy smiled.

'We had a bit of a drink the other night and cleared the air. He's pretty much a blokes bloke mind you, but with a dark and deadly secret though?'

The Chief seemed to nod, raise an eyebrow.

'Well, turns out, when he was in his teens he …'

She looked over her shoulder.

'He used to be a train spotter. Can you believe it? Bottle-bottom glasses and waxy anorak. Clipboard, leaky biro. The lot.'

The lads seemed to chuckle at that.

'I know. Much more embarrassing than being a post-op tranny. No doubt about that.'

She closed her eyes and slowly felt the joint, the job, the operation, life, wash over her. A weight seemed to lift from her shoulders. She opened her eyes and looked up at the stars. They sparkled. Really sparkled. She grinned. They seemed to be smiling at her. Winking. Dancing.

She decided it was time for bed.

'Evenin' all,' she said and gave a little salute before getting unsteadily to her feet. 'Let's be careful out there.'

And then she collapsed on the floor in a heap.

***

Matt Cane had lost count of how many push ups he'd done. In fact, he'd lost track of time completely. He was in 'the zone'. A magical place way from all of his troubles. In the womb of red mist, consumed by anger and hate.

He kept repeating his mantra: 'Fuck em all. Fuck em all. Fuck.Em.All.'

This was the best way for him to focus when he was stressed, under pressure. He'd learnt it from a tattoo-latticed English bank robber called Blue Dobson. A real psycho that one for sure. Cane had met the guy when he was researching a role of a soccer hooligan in a cockney gangster film he'd made with Toby Wills, the guy that used to own the mansion he now lived in. He was angrily dragged out of the zone when Rossiter walked down the steps into the basement.

Rossiter sniffed. The air was stale, sweaty. At times like this, he was glad of his lifelong sinus condition. The fully-fitted gym was in the basement of the mansion and Cane seemed to spend more time down there than he did rehearsing for whatever bloated piece of Hollywood twaddle he was due to be overpaid to appear in next.

Rossiter was approaching sixty and couldn't wait for his early retirement. He'd been a butler for over thirty ears and there had been mostly good times but some bad. However, the last six months with Matt Cane had been the closest thing to hell he'd experienced since the jungles of Korea.

He coughed.

Nothing.

Coughed again.

Cane stopped his exercises in a ridiculously uncomfortable looking position.

'Would sir be preferring to lunch here or on the veranda?' said Rossiter. He had to raise his voice since a Public Enemy 'song' was playing at full volume.

Cane gave Rossiter a glare.

'Don't be an asshole, Rossiter,' said Cane. He sniffed his armpits. Inhaled. 'Harvey's on his way. You've got fifteen minutes. Chill the martini glasses now. The special recipe. You know the drill.'

'Yes, sir,' said Rossiter, walking up the stairs.

'And let me know if she gets here early. Okay?'

'Sir.'

'Faggot.'

'Fight The Powers That Be,' sang Rossiter, under his breath

***

Marty had always tried to be a tolerant non-judgmental type. Take people as you find them. Live and let live, to each his own and the like. A person's race, religion and or whatever had never mattered to him. He'd never been keen on poofs when he was younger, mind you but these days he wasn't that bothered either way. Let them get on with it. He felt he'd matured. Mellowed. Become more centred.

But there was something about mime artists that did his napper in. He always wanted to grab them by the throat and make them squeal. It wasn't just the face make-up, although that helped; even when he was a kid, he'd hated clowns. Been a bit scared of them, if he was honest. But mime artists just wound him up something rotten. Especially that walking against the wind thing. Really did his napper in.

Today there were hundreds of them up and down the Acton High Street handing out flyers for some shitty fun fair that was being set up on Shepherd's Bush Green. He resisted his violent urges and walked past them, chewing the inside of his cheek. When he walked up to the back door of La Salsa he was fuming.

And then it got worse.

Baghead Berry, a snotty faced ratboy in a ragged black hoodie was pissing against the club door and Marty Cook quickly lost the plot.

'You slag!' he shouted and grabbed Baghead by the neck. Before he knew what he was doing, he had repeatedly slammed the emaciated teenager's head against the metal reinforced door. He let go and the youth's unconscious body slid down onto the pavement.

'Cobblers,' he whispered to himself when he realised that the youth was unconscious and bleeding. He'd gone too far. Again. He picked up the skinny waster with ease and hauled him into a nearby wheelie-bin. Slammed down the lid. Best place for the likes of him.

Marty quickly unlocked the door and opened up the club. He switched off the alarm and shuffled as quickly up the concrete steps as he could before opening the door that led to the bar.

'The things you see on television these days,' purred Veronica, who was sat at the bar, looking up at the CCTV. 'Corrupts the minds of the sensitive.' Her dark eyes glistened. She was wearing a black roll neck sweater, black leggings and high heeled boots. Very exotic. Every inch the Latino, thought Marty.

'I'm cream crackered,' said Marty. 'Getting too old for that sort of carrying on.'

He collapsed onto a small wooden chair, which rattled the empty glasses on the neighbouring table.

'Me too,' said Veronica. She reached into the fridge behind the bar and plucked out a couple of bottles of Pellegrino. 'But growing old is better than the alternative.'

Marty laughed. Veronica was a stunning looking woman, no matter what her age was. Tall, hair in a classic black bob. A slash of crimson lipstick. Nail varnish the same shade. Dark, piercing eyes. And although her Spanish accent was faint it still gave her a certain … frisson.

'Too much of a misspent youth in my case, I reckon,' he said. His breath was steadying.

'Better to regret something you have done than to regret something you haven't done,' said Veronica with a wink.

Marty was starting to chill out again. He liked to meet up with Veronica at the club at least once a week for a session but he'd been too busy recently. It would be good to be back in the saddle, though.

He kept an eye on the television screen behind the bar. The CCTV outside the club had picked up a couple more hoodies that were shuffling about outside. Handing baggies over to equally dodgy types. It made his heart sink.

Veronica followed his gaze.

'Two legged rats,' she said.

'Yeah, there are too many of them round this shit-hole for my liking,' he said.

Marty took the bottle of water from Veronica. Ripped the top off and downed it in one.

He looked around the club. La Salsa was a class joint, for sure. He'd spent a fortune on interior decoration and Veronica was one of the best dance teachers in Europe. She'd even been in an award winning film about the history of the tango, apparently. Not that he'd seen it. He was more of a HBO man; *Boardwalk Empire, Deadwood, The Sopranos.*

Yep, the club had the potential to be one of the best Latino dance clubs in West London, if not the whole country. But stuck in this crappy, dying part of the city there was no way it was going to attract the right crowd, no matter how much they tried.

'Come on,' she said, waggling her fingers. 'Dance away the stress.'

Por Una Cabeza started up.

'Okey dokey, pig in pokey,' said Marty. He straightened his red velvet shirt and the Tango began.

***

Although he'd never been particularly fond of The Muppets, kicking one of them in the bollocks still made Kenny feel a bit guilty. But Fozzie Bear had really had it coming this time. What a twat he was. When Kenny had called into Toffy's Offy on Churchfield Road for a sausage roll, Fozzie had been stood, staggering in the queue as drunk as a skunk, swigging from a can of Special Brew and shouting his mouth off about 'Slaggy' Thatcher and how she wasn't the innocent that she'd made herself out to be.

Toffy himself – a corpulent slug of a man with a permanently constipated expression – was behind the counter, perched on a dishevelled armchair doing Sudoku after Sudoku, seemingly oblivious to the Muppet's ranting. But the bloke in the filthy Fozzie Bear costume just wouldn't shut up, though, and to make matters worse, when Kenny eventually left the shop, he saw that Fozzie's mates were pissing against the side of Kenny's new BMW. Then Fozzie staggered out and banged into Kenny, forcing him to drop the jumbo sausage rolls he'd just bought. So Kenny Rogan had piled in there and Fozzie Bear was now whimpering on the floor.

Sweating more than a tad after flooring Fozzie, Kenny looked around at the other Muppets.

'Well? Anyone else fancy their chances?'

'Not me mate,' said the Swedish Chef, his shaky hands held high, accent broad Brummie. 'Never liked him anyway. Shit sax player, too.'

He burped and wandered into Keith & Babs' Kebab Shop. The other Muppets shuffled in after him, heads down.

'I'm friggin starving,' said Miss Piggy, wrapping her arm around a wobbly Gonzo. 'But make sure they don't put any of that red cabbage on my kebab. I don't do veg.'

A wheezing Fozzie grabbed Kenny by the ankles. Held out a business card. 'Listen mush, if you're ever looking for band for a charity gig let me know, eh?'

SPLIT UP THE MONEY

If DS Ronnie Burke squeezed the rubber ball any harder he was sure either it or he would explode. His wife had got it for him after his first heart attack scare and it was supposed to help him manage his stress levels, but it certainly wasn't doing the trick at the moment. Matt Cane was just the sort of person that you wanted to punch and punch and punch. If it wasn't his body movements it was the shite that came out of his mouth.

Cane was dressed in black with black wraparound shades, pacing the police station's grubby interview room. He stopped and help up a finger.

'Picture this,' said Matt Cane. 'A galaxy, far far away. A …'

'I've never seen *Star Wars*,' said Burke.

Cane looked aghast.

'But, how, what …'

'I was sixteen when the film came out,' said Burke. 'Too old for that load of kids' space-man cobblers, eh? I had a job. Was shagging a mate's mother. Listening to The Stranglers. Why would I care about kids' films?'

Cane was like statue. His mouth creaked open. 'Yes, but George Lucas' vision is …'

'Yeah, yeah. A parable or something. A satire of western cobblers and the like. Heard it all before. Still a kids' film eh?' said Burke. 'Not exactly Samuel Becket, is it?'

'But … but …'

'Yeah, anyway. Your little baby books have been stolen and apparently someone can sell that cobblers for a mint.'

Cane struggles to contain his temper. Closes his eyes and counts to ten.

'Dude, could you translate that into English?' he said.

***

'Let's get ready to rumble,' said Scopey, in an annoying Donald Duck voice.

Scopey was one of those people that Be-Bop just want to twat and twat and twat. He was an itchy, twitchy smack-head who peppered his conversations with impersonations of cartoon characters.

'Awld on,' said Binky, looking suitably pissed off.

He moved the pub's tables into a semi-circle. Patsy, the pasty faced landlady, glanced up from her Sudoku when one of the legs squeaked on the floorboards. Glared. Binky forced a smile and looked like he's having a stroke.

'Ta for your help, Be-Bop,' he said. 'Appreciate it.'

'Nothing I can do,' said Be-Bop. 'Got to keep hold of this.'

He tapped the camcorder. 'Don't want anyone thieving it, do I?'

Binky looked around at The Fisherman's Arms' geriatric customers.

'Yeah, that will be right,' he said.

'You're a big lad, Binky,' said Be-Bop. 'You can manage.'

And he was big. Massive. A behemoth with a shaved head and a face latticed with scars.

'Ready when you are,' said Scopey. He wiped his snotty nose with his shirt sleeve and did a more than passable Woody Woodpecker laugh.

Be-Bop switched on the camcorder.

'Ladies first,' said Binky, amping up his Glasgow accent for the camera.

'Yabba dabba do,' said Scopey.

He grunted as he slammed a fist into Binky's guts.

'Ow!'

Binky grasped Scopey fist in his catcher's mitt sized paws, turned to the camera and winked. He chuckled as he crushed the hand, the cracking of bone quickly drowned out by Scopey's screams.

Scopey crumbled onto the sticky pub floor. Binky stood on Scopey's knee until it popped and Scopey passed out.

A couple of booze hounds sitting at a table by the fruit machine furtively looked over, Binky turns to Be-Bop with a shit eating grin, gave the double thumbs up and took a bow.

'How was that, chief?'

'Good one,' said Be-Bop.

He switched off the camcorder.

'Piece of piss,' said Binky.

Be-Bop leaned over and stuffed a handful of notes into Scopey's shirt pocket.

'Pleasure doing business with you,' he said, his back creaking as he straightened up.

He walked over to the bar and slid a twenty pound note over to Patsy.

'It'll take more than that to clean the carpet,' she said, stabbing a pinkie toward Scopey. 'He's pissed himself.'

Be-Bop bit his tongue and peeled another twenty from his expenses roll.

'That do you?'

'It'll have to,' she said, pushing it into the back pocket of her jeans.

'I'm off for a Gypsy's Kiss,' said Binky.

Be-Bop finish off his Red Bull as Binky headed off to the little boys' room. Patsy turned up the TV and the theme from *Flog It!* played as Be-Bop left the dingy pub and stepped into the bright afternoon light.

The street was cluttered with extras from *The Walking Dead*. A gangling postman staggered towards him, changed direction and then shuffled off across the street, narrowly avoiding being splattered by a dusty ice cream van which pulled up outside the betting shop, the driver singing along to a Sham 69 song. An old woman ran her tartan shopping trolley over Be-Bop's foot.

'Bugger off,' she said, as he yelped.

'We hittin' the road, chief?' said Binky, pulling up his fly and sniffing his fingers.

'Yeah, let's get out of this dump,' said Be-Bop.

His phone buzzed and he took it out. It was a text message from Father Tim Cook.

'Jesus Christ,' he said. 'Or close enough.'

***

A bitter winter evening bled into night and the winter moon hung fat and gibbous as Father Tim blasted Bilko Sanderson's head from his shoulders and watched it roll across the snow smothered ground. The splashes of blood looked black in the stark moonlight.

A smirk crawled across Tim's face. He had never liked Bilko. Really couldn't stand the big mouthed twat, to be honest. So, this was more a pleasure than a chore.

A murder of crows scattered and sliced across the white moon, as the purr of an approaching Mercedes grew to a roar. The black car screeched to a stop in a nearby alleyway, between Tony Cook's gentleman's club, The Blue Lagoon, and a former Methodist church that had been converted into a heavy metal club. The driver got out. He was wearing a long black overcoat and a wide-brimmed hat, and Gregor looked like a shadow as he cut through the deserted car park. Snow began to fall like confetti.

Tim pulled a black woollen hat over his shaved head.

'Nice of you to join us,' he said.

'It was the *X-Factor* final,' said Gregor. 'Tense stuff.'

Gregor and Father Tim took Bilko's body by the ankles and dragged the corpse towards the dark and dingy alley, leaving behind a snaking trail of blood. They pulled Bilko up to the car, illuminated by the light from a stained glass window, and opened the boot. With a grunt, they hauled the cadaver inside and slammed the lid shut.

'Let's get moving,' said Tim.

They got into the car and Gregor started up the engine.

'Fancy a little night music?' said Gregor.

He clicked on the radio and Massive Attack's *Karmacoma* played.

'At little shite music more like it,' said Tim.

Gregor snorted and pulled out of the alleyway.

'You've really got the music taste of a man of a certain age,' said Gregor.

'I am a man of a certain age,' said Tim.

Gregor chuckled.

'How may more on the fuck-it list, anyway?' said Gregor, as they turned into a darkened side street.

'Only a couple left now,' said Tim. 'Next one should be the hat-trick.'

They cruised along until they stopped outside a closed up fish and chip shop. There were graffiti stained metal shutters over the front door and windows but The Small Fry still did a roaring trade during the day.

'All of them easy as this one?'

'No, unfortunately not. One of them could be a right twat to do away with.'

'Will we need help?'

'Nah, Kenny Rogan's not the man he used to be, thank fuck. But he was a right head the ball in his day.'

They got out of the car and Tim took out his phone. Dialled.

'Magda,' he said. 'We're here.'

After a moment the shutters to the chip shop's door were rolled up. A tall woman with a ginger beehive and a fake leopard skin coat stepped out.

'Cold enough to freeze a monkey's bollocks off out here,' she said in a hard scouse accent. 'get him in.'

Gregor opened the boot and he and Tim picked up Bilko's body and carried it into the café.

'Ta much,' said Magda as she held the door open. 'This'll keep us supplied with battered sausage for a couple of weeks. Or more. Fancy something to eat while you're here?'

'Strangely, I'm not that peckish at the moment,' said Tim. 'What about you, Gregor?'

'Oh, yes. I could eat a horse.'

'Well, let's just hope that's all it is,' said Tim.

***

'Well, I've seen healthier sights in the morgue,' said Ronnie.

He was sat on a wobbly stool in one of the police station's interview rooms, which was so spartan he assumed some ponce on the telly would probably describe as minimalist but anyone else would have called undecorated.

The green paint on the door was peeling. The grubby grey walls were stained with bodily fluids, graffiti and spots of Blue Tac. The heating was broken and an old electric fan heater belted out blasts of hot air intermittently. Still, it was one of the few places you could get some privacy these days. The nick was riddled with security cameras now.

Niki Scrace was sat opposed it him. She had draped an old tartan blanket over her shoulders and was shivering as she held a mug of green tea in both hands. A CD player someone had once 'rescued' from a crime scene was belting out the hits of the eighties and Dexy's Midnight Runners were inviting all and sundry to *Come On Eileen*.

'Are you sure the quack said you're alright?' said Ronnie.

Scrace sipped the green tea that he had made her and tried to avoid grimacing. Ronnie had put a ton of sugar in it.

'Yeah, I just need to take it easy for a while. I was a bit daft hitting the wacky-backy so much so soon after the operation,' she said.

'Personally, I reckon the odd joint is fair enough herbal remedy, every now and again,' said Ronnie. He drained the last of his black coffee. 'But at the right time and a place, though.'

'True, true. Any news on the comic book robbery?'

'Naw, but that actor bloke is going mental. He's got some flash Hollywood lawyer on the line to us night and day. A bird, would you believe. Talks like a country and western singer.'

'All lawyers are count-ry and western singers,' said Scrace.

'True, true Barney McGrew We'll soon find out how much of a one she is, anyway. She's coming down to see us later today, if you're up for it.'

'Wouldn't miss it for the world. Anything else happening?'

'Well, that truck driver may be a person of interest as they say on the goggle box,' said Ronnie.

'Why's that?' She pressed the mug against her cheek.

'Well, he's a bloke by the name of Kenny Rogan. Heard of him?'

'Can't say I have.'

'Well, once upon a crime, donkey's years ago, he used to be one of Mad Tony Cook's boys. You must have heard of him?'

'Yeah, he was a bit of a London landmark, I think.'

'Oh yes, like the plague and the Blitz'.

'So, do you think this might be a dodgy insurance scam?' said Scrace, struggling to finish of her tea.

'Well, you never know. But it seems a bit too obvious, though. I can't imagine any of the Cooks shitting on their own doorstep, as it were. They're many things but they're not stupid.'

Ronnie finished his coffee and struggled off the stool. Stretched his legs.

'Should we drag Kenny Rogan in again? Give him a heavy-duty grilling?' said Scrace.

'Maybe. But first off I want to see what Aldo Calvino's got to say,' said Ronnie.

'Who's he when he's at home.'

'He's one of the biggest fences in the city. Literally. A right fat twat, he is,' said Ronnie, scratching his own beer gut. 'Something as big and valuable as those comics is sure to go through him. The more specialised and obscure the product, the more likely it is that Aldo will be involved in shifting it. Well, either him or a geezer called Ron Moody but Moody seems to have gone underground. Quite apt really, since he looks like a vampire.'

'Will this Aldo help us out, though. I can't imagine he's what you'd call a good citizen?'

'Oh, yes. For sure. He owes me, big time. The numpties at immigration have been all over this little Peruvian bint he's been knocking off and I'm keeping them off her back while she's on hers.'

Scrace supressed a sigh.

'What do we do, then? Drag him in and put the thumb-screws on him or go to see him?'

'Well, I'd normally pop in to see him, to be honest. His gaff is a bit of a dump but it's a bit of an Aladdin's cave and he's usually got some tidy booze and knocked-off clobber hanging around there. Trouble is, I can't seem to track him down. It's like he's disappeared off the face of the earth. Both his mobile numbers are dead and so is his landline.'

'Another fence gone underground.'

***

Father Tim sighed. Sighed again. Harrumphed. Made an annoying clicking sound with his tongue. He stood with his hands on his hips, shaking his head, flaky scalp snowing on his shoulders. He was wearing a worn Afghan coat over a black leather jacket. His paint flecked jeans were tucked into scuffed cowboy boots that had metal toe caps.

'This is a pain in the arse it really is,' he rasped.

'You're telling me,' Be-Bop said. 'Moving dead bodies isn't exactly something I'm prone to do of a cold winter morning. And couldn't you have brought a bigger carpet, by the way?'

They'd wrapped Wolfie Amerigo's body in a grubby, fluffy white rug that Tim had brought with him but Amerigo's legs were sticking out of the bottom. A dirty big toe stuck out of an Argyle sock.

'I'm not exactly an expert on this kind of thing, you know?' said Tim.

'Who is? But his stinky feet are a bit conspicuous, don't you think? A bit of a clue as to what's inside the rug.'

'Can't we just cover them with something?'

'Like what?'

'What about a bin liner?'

Be-Bop sighed and looked around.

'Does it look like he uses a bin?' he said.

'He must have something.'

'Yeah, maybe.'

Be-Bop bent down and peered in the cupboard under the sink.

'Jeez, that's not a sight or smell to help my dodgy guts.' he tried not to gag.

'I'd help you look but with my knees …'said Tim.

'Hold on a bit,' said Be-Bop, through clenched teeth.

He held his breath and dug into the back of the cupboard. He eventually found a roll of black bin liners and pulled it out.

'This should do the trick,' he said.

He wrapped it around the corpse's feet.

'See if you can see some gaffer tape,' said Be-Bop. 'Or something to fasten it with.'

'Gaffer tape?'

'He used to be a drummer, didn't he? They always have gaffer tape.'

Tim opened up a drawer.

'Now, now, now, look at this beauty,' he said.

He took out a Luger. Pointed it at the door.

'For fuck's sake,' said Be-Bop. 'Is that the real thing?'

'Dunno if it's an original but it certainly looks functional. Probably worth a fair bit, anyway.'

Tim smirked and shoved the gun into the back of his jeans.

He rummaged in the drawer and took out a roll of scotch tape. 'This do?' he said.

'It'll have to.'

They wrapped the bin liner tightly around Amerigo's legs. Tim ripped the tape open with his teeth and wrapped a fair amount of tape around the bin liner and put the rest around the carpet.

'Ready?' said Be-Bop.

'And steady,' said Tim.

Be-Bop peeked out of the front door and saw Tim's white van, the back doors wide open. No one else around.

'Heel and toe and off we go,' said Tim.

They picked up the carpet. Tim groaned.

'Jeez, he's a heavy fucker for such a little bloke,' he said.

They headed toward the van.

'This is what a diet of Special Brew and takeaway grub does for you,' said Tim.

'So speaks Mr Body Beautiful,' said Be-Bop with a gasp.

Tim slammed the back doors shut. Be-Bop looked back at the bungalow.

'Are we going to clean up in the caravan first or piss off?' he said.

'Let's lock it up and get the fuck out of here,' said Tim.

He took a padlock from his coat pocket and locked the front door.

'Should do the trick for now,' he said.

They got in the van and drove out of the caravan site and out of town.

Tim switched on the radio. It was playing Kajagoogo.

'Lord help us,' said Be-Bop.

He changed stations and found a phone-in talk show. The host and callers were discussing the upcoming elections. It was getting pretty heated.

Tim slowed at a zebra crossing and drummed his fingers on the steering wheel as an old woman with a tartan shopping trolley doddered across the road.

'I don't follow politics myself,' said Be-Bop. 'Which party is this bloke in?'

'GBIP,' said Tim. 'Not that I know much about them.'

'They're a bunch of tossers, I think,' said Be-Bop.

'Aren't they all?'

'Probably. People put too much faith in politicians to sort out their lives.'

'Aye. Life's all about playing a bad hand of cards well,' said Tim.

'You're not far wrong," said Be-Bop.

Tim slammed in a Pink Floyd CD and they drove in silence, listening to the music until they approached a dilapidated farmhouse with a small pigpen in front of it.

'I assume this is Jed Bramble's place, then?' said Be-Bop.

'The self-same. Know Jed? He's a musician.'

'Can't say that I do.'

'He used to sing all them Irish rebel songs,' said Tim.

'Which part of Ireland is he from?'

'He isn't. Never set foot in the country.'

'There's a lot of it about,' said Be-Bop.

As they parked in front of the farmhouse a stocky man in jeans and a striped pajama top came out, carrying a sawn off shotgun and pulling on an anorak. He was bald with massive ginger sideburns. He squinted at Tim and gave a gummy grin. He leaned the shotgun against the wall and took a pair of false teeth out of his coat pocket. Jammed them in his mouth.

Tim got out of the van first.

'Well, you daft old bugger. You're still not dead?' he said.

'You never know,' said Jed. 'Could well be but no one's bothered to tell me.'

It started to rain as Be-Bop got out of the van.

'Who this, then?' said Jed.

'Be-Bop De Luca. One of our friends from the north,' said Tim.

'Ah, I used to know your dad,' said Jed. 'Canny Joanna player in his day. Didn't he win *Opportunity Knocks*?'

'*New Faces*,' said Be-Bop. 'Twice.'

'That's right,' said Jed. 'And you did *Junior Showtime*. Lost to a banjo player with a squint.'

'Trina Macaroni won, didn't she?' said Tim. 'She was probably shagging Glyn Pool.'

He grinned.

'Thanks for the memories,' said Be-Bop.

'Better come on in,' said Jed. 'What have you got me to gargle?'

Tim took a Tesco carrier bag filled with chinking bottles out of the van.

'The loot of all the world,' he said.

'I'd settle for a bottle of Grants,' said Jed.

'What about the, you know?' Be-Bop nodded toward the back of the van.

'Don't you worry your head about that. I'll feed my little beauties later. Let them build up a bit of an appetite,' said Jed. He licked his lips and nodded toward the pig pen.

Be-Bop followed Tim and Jed into the cottage and was more than somewhat taken aback by its appearance. The place was pristine, almost antiseptic. The exact opposite of its scruffy exterior. Minimalist and white, like the heist scene in the first *Mission Impossible* film. There were two black leather sofas, a stainless steel fridge, a drinks cabinet and a matt black table. On one wall, a projector was showing a Blue Ray version of *North By North West*.

Jed walked over to the table and put down the carrier bag, carefully, delicately. He looked contended.

'We'll all be partaking, I assume,' he said.

'I am,' said Tim. 'Dunno about Be-Bop, though. I hear he's gone all soft and southern on us.'

'I'm in. I could do with a little eye-opener,' said Be-Bop.

Jed picked up a remote control and turned off the film's sound. Another click and they were listening to The Dubliners.

'Is your dad still alive and kickin' then?' said Jed.

He went over to a drinks cabinet and took out a couple of tumblers.

'Very much so. Kickin' off when he's on the whisky,' said Be-Bop.

'Where's he living now?' said Tim. 'He's not still in Seatown, is he?'

Be-Bop sat down on one of the sofas.

'Naw, he moved to Alston?'

'Where the frig is Alston, when it's at home?' said Jed. 'Never heard of the place.'

'It's the highest market town in Britain, apparently.'

'Still no clue,' said Jed.

'It's in the back of beyond, middle of nowhere. Some interbred, sheep shagging bit of Cumbria,' said Tim.

'You live and learn,' said Jed.

He handed out the drinks. Be-Bop took a sip, gagged. Waited a moment and knocked it back in one.

'So, any idea who croaked Wolfie Amerigo, then?' said Jed.

'Dunno. Not a clue,' said Father Tim.

'I suppose it's pointless asking if he had any enemies,' said Be-Bop.

'You could pick a name at random from the phone book,' said Tim.

'Do people still have phone books?' said Jed. 'I've everything I need here.'

He pulled out an iPhone. Tapped it. Smirked.

Be-Bop's guts burned. He gulped and downed his drink.

Jed filled up his tumbler.

'So, who do you reckon the most likely suspect is?' he said. 'One of Satan's Souls?'

'A bit of a coup, eh? Could be,' said Tim. 'Though as far as I'm aware Wolfie's been little more than a figurehead for a few years now. And his body was so wrecked it was only a matter of time before he croaked on some dodgy Feta?'

'The cheese?' said Be-Bop, confused.

'Amphetamine,' said Tim. 'You not down with the kids?'

'Not a lot,' said Be-Bop.

He lay back on the sofa and went to sleep.

***

'Kung Fu. Karate. Judo. Aikido,' said Matt Cane, as he practised his moves in front of the bedroom mirror. 'Jeet Kune – motherfucking – Do! I am the master of all martial arts!'

He assumed a martial arts pose. Then another. He lunged at the mirror.

'Who is the goddamn master?' he screamed.

'Oh, you are Mr Cane. Most indubitably,' said a stern faced Rossiter. 'God, and indeed, damn.'

Ride Of The Valkyries blasted out of the ludicrously expensive sound system as Cane plucked a pair of black nunchucks from the back of his black boxer shorts, twirling them around until they were inches from Rossiter's beaky nose.

'Oh, very good, sir,' purred Rossiter. 'Very impressive. Quite balletic.'

Rossiter had always considered himself to be a master of self-control. Stoic, if need be. But he was having great difficulty controlling his temper and even greater problems resisting the urge to burst out laughing.

'Pass me that mascara,' said Matt Cane, not taking his eyes from the wardrobe mirror.

Rossiter did as he was told but avoided looking at Cane, who was dressed only in his tight satin boxer shorts, in the eye or anywhere else for that matter. Cane started chanting some Native American war chant and began painting his eyes black in preparation for putting on a black leather mask that was perched on top of a bed post. He'd been chuntering on about something or other for what seemed like an eternity though Rossiter, as ever, hadn't really been paying attention.

'I mean, Bale. For fucks sake. A Limey. And now Affleck? Pure balsa wood. I do not believe it,' muttered Cane.

'Indeed. A tragedy,' said Rossiter, stifling a yawn and not having a clue what Cane was prattling on about.

Cane looked at himself in the mirror and seemed pleased with what he saw. Patted his crotch. Grinned.

'The Dark Knight will surely rise tonight,' he yelled, punching the air.

Rossiter shuffled uncomfortably.

'Ha!' yelled Cane, and then he somersaulted onto the four-poster bed, quickly assuming some sort of martial arts pose. He held the pose, expressionless, for a full two minutes while Rossiter bit the inside of his cheeks to avoid letting out a full-on guffaw.

The doorbell chimed the theme tune to *The A Team*, much to Rossiter's relief.

'Okay, let's do it,' said Cane. He jumped off the bed and Rossiter opened the bedroom door.

'Ready when you are,' he said.

Cane rushed out of the bedroom, vaulted over the handrail and landed in the hall below, just as the doorbell rang again.

'What's the goddamn rush!' he screamed, holding his landing pose.

He opened the front door to Stephanie Harvey, the tall, blue-eyed Texan who worked as his lawyer. Harvey wore a dark blue Armani suit, a bootlace tie and a Stetson with a brim as wide as her grin.

'Well, good afternoon to you, Mr Cane,' drawled Harvey, taking off her Stetson. 'And how may I be of your assistance?'

'I want you to kick some ass, farm girl,' said Cane, not noticing Harvey chew her bottom lip. 'Some chicken shit Limey ass.'

***

Marty was sure he was going to puke any minute now. Whether he had his eyes open or closed the world still kept spinning round. He had no idea how long he'd been on the Ferris wheel but he couldn't wait to get off. Veronica had been talking ten to the dozen for what seemed like an eternity and he was losing track of what she was going on about.

'And there are families and communities all living there in the sewers,' said Veronica

'In Las Vegas?' said Marty. He mumbled as he spoke believing that if he opened his mouth wide he'd projectile vomit all over the fairground below.

'Yeah, must be crazy, eh?'

'Yeah, mental.'

She chuckled.

'Come on, Marty. Open your eyes,' said Veronica. 'The view is wicked.'

She said the word 'wicked' in a fake cockney accent which was made even more grating by her supressed giggle.

'You're alright, sweetheart,' he said. 'I'm happy enough as I am. Enjoy yourself. Fill your boots.'

He heard the sound of creaking metal and felt the motion of the big wheel slowly descending. His guts following only minutes after. He started counting backwards from one hundred. It stopped at twenty-two. His stomach lurched.

'We're here,' said Veronica, patting his sweaty paw. Marty peeled himself out of the metal wagon and onto the waste ground where Big Mack's Fun Fair had been set up. A group of teenagers rushed past him and sent him staggering forward. Veronica caught him before he hit the ground.

'Slow deep breaths,' said Veronica.

Marty looked around. His senses were overloaded. Flashing lights. Loud music. The smell of hot-dogs, candy floss, chips.

'Fancy a cheeseburger?' said Veronica.

The world spun around and Marty ran into a corner near the Ghost Train. Spewed his ring up.

'Better out than in,' said a stumpy Santa Clause that was smoking a match sized roll-up. He wandered off singing 'Oh, Ruby! Don't take your knickers down.'

It was Marty's own fault for mentioning that bucket list thing, of course. He'd seen a film about it with Jack Nicholson. How some people make a list of things that people want to do before they die. Veronica had come up with a litany of suggestions for her list.

Marty had said that he preferred the idea of a 'fuck it list.' Things that he hoped never to have to do before he died. Like backpack across the outback or parachute jump. Or go on a big wheel. Anything to do with heights in fact. Marty hated high places. He got vertigo in thick socks.

Veronica had then decided that he should confront his fears or some such positive-thinking cobblers and cajoled him into a trip to the fun fair. Now he was spewing his ring up in front of a handful of giggling Goths. And Marty hated Goths almost as much as he hated mime artists. Probably the patchouli oil.

'Let's go for coffee,' said Veronica, leading him toward a nearby café.

'I'd rather have a proper drink,' said Marty, feeling a little better. 'My mum always says that a G&T was the best thing for an upset stomach.'

'Well, there's one of those fun pubs over there?'

'Not so sure I'm a fun person at the moment, Veronica. I'd prefer an old man's pub full of sour-faced, saggy-bollocked underachievers drinking flat bitter. The whole Brit Shit experience.'

'I know just the place,' said Veronica. 'You can even get a pickled egg to fire up your ulcer.'

***

By early evening Be-Bop and Father Tim were sitting in Astros Wine Bar, an overpriced, up its own arse boozer on the edge of Surbiton. All red leather and chrome, it looked like an eighties porn film set. Be-Bop was staring behind the bar at a stained glass recreation of the famed poster of the female tennis player scratching her arse that many a teenage boy had on their wall in the seventies.

'I remember splashing out on one of them posters back in the day,' said Tim. 'And those old *Top Of The Pops* LPs. Remember them? Dodgy cover version of current hits and that.'

'I worked with a bloke who was a session musician on a few of those albums. Made a packet, apparently. More than a lot of the original musicians by the sound of it.'

'Yeah? You live and learn,' said Tim, flicking though his battered brown wallet.

'Strapped for cash?' said Be-Bop.

'Got a bit of plastic but not much mooching around money. They do CASHBACK here, though. Comes in handy.'

'Remember cheque guarantee cards? They were a life saver when you had no folding money and were sobering up.'

'They were alright in the restaurants and off-licences but not much cop in the pubs. Pubs never took cheques. Not round here, anyway.'

'Aye, but there was a way around that. If you went to the travel agents you could use them to buy foreign cash. Then you went to another travel agents and changed the foreign currency for English dosh.'

'I never thought about that. Must have lost a fair bit on the exchange rate, though?'

'Oh aye. But the bank charges were the real killer,' said Be-Bop. 'I can see why the banks stopped them, though.'

A shard of light sliced through the curtains picking out the flecks of dust that hung in the air. The music stopped and Tim and Be-Bop sat in silence. After a while, Be-Bop noticed that Tim had fallen asleep. The calm was interrupted by a loud braying voice.

'This is only the beginning for GBIP. One day our supporters will fill stadia and I'll need octopi to shake hands with all the well-wishers,' said Tarquin Farrago. He was wearing a dinner jacket and holding a massive cigar. A red faced man in a shiny supermarket suit shuffled beside him, nodding like one of those toy dogs everyone's dad used to have in the back of their car in the seventies.

The word stadia was enough to drag Tim from his sleep by his lapels. Immediately alert, he leapt to his feet and roughly took hold of Farrago.

'Stadia! Stadia! Now, let's, for a moment, leave aside the … banality of using Latin plurals on English words with Latin roots – would you, for example, do the same with English words with French roots? Or Malaysian? What's the Malaysian plural of Ketchup, eh? But even if you follow this pathetic logic, the plural of Octopus would be 'octuped' since the word is derived from the Greek. But I'm sure you know that, eh?'

Tim let go of Farrago's throat just enough for him to croak: 'Oh, yes. Oh, kay.'

'No, I suspect you don't. But then I've always considered you to be the sort who knows the price of a few things and the value of nothing. Even when I was unlucky enough to have you as my primary school teacher. Which is why it comes as no great surprise to me that the GBIP is your particular political party of choice.'

Tim sat back down and knocked back his drink.

Flustered, sweating and shaking, Farrago scuttled out of the door, his lackey trailing behind him.

***

Richard Sanderson, the gangling long-haired wanker with the ratty goatee, was a right annoying twat, no doubt about it. He was the one that, if Kenny was the sort of man he had been twenty years before, well, he would have beaten ten buckets of shit out of him. But his mate, the one with the rubbery lips and floppy blonde hair, he would have been the one that Kenny would have had to be stopped from killing. Luckily, rubber-lips had pissed off home and left his long-haired mate to shout his mouth off. And shout he did. So much so that Kenny reached the end of his tether.

One hard kick and the long-haired layabout was tumbling down the stairs. He was nothing but a long drink of water, a skinny waste of space and Kenny knew he shouldn't have let the big-mouthed pillock get his goat but it had been a long, hard week and it was only bloody Tuesday.

Richard was always annoying, though. It came with the territory. He came into La Salsa at least once a week, out of his face on Colombian marching powder, shouting his mouth off and throwing his money about.

Anyone else would have got a good kicking in the alleyway at the back of the club but Richard was the estranged son of Terry Cook. Terry was now in the nick but he was the owner of many a slot machine emporium and massage parlour in that part of the city, and was a class 'A' gangster from the golden-olden days and maybe even before. He'd been Terry's secret son until his brother Tony had run into him and his mother during the infamous search for the missing briefcase. He was Marty and Father Tim's half-brother and Richard knew that meant he was pretty much untouchable. Smug twat.

In the past Kenny hadn't given a shit about Richard's carryings-on, though. He'd usually ignored the little shit with little effort but tonight, well Kenny's string had snapped and Richard was now laying at the bottom of a flight of stairs with his head out of the door on Acton High Street.

'Think he's alright,' said Kenny.

'Would you be?' said Turban Ted, the only Sikh Teddy Boy in the vicinity. 'But you'd better hope he is cos if any of the Cooks find out about this, you're in the shit one way or another.'

Kenny was feeling hot under the collar of his monkey suit. His hands were clammy and his heart was beating ten to the dozen. He'd just about made amends with the Cook family, after losing the aforementioned briefcase after a heist went pear shaped and he'd known his survival had been a close thing. He supposed that was one of the reasons why he'd gone legit. Or tried to.

He carefully eased down the stairs. Loomed over Richard's prone form.

Richard just looked like he was sleeping off a big boozing session. Which, in many ways he was, although involuntarily.

Kenny bent down and furtively touched Richard's forehead.

'Well?' said Ted, from the safety of the top of the flight of stairs. 'How is he?'

'Seems alive to me,' said Kenny. 'I mean, I'm no Doctor House but aren't corpses supposed to be cold?'

'I think it takes longer than that, Kenny,' said Ted. 'Maybe check his pulse.'

'How do I do that, then?' said Kenny.

Ted slapped his forehead. 'Haven't you seen a dead body before?' he said.

'Yeah, of course. But there was usually no doubt about whether or not they were worm-food.'

'Well, I dunno,' said Ted. 'Just grab his wrists or something.'

Kenny took Richard by the wrist but he really didn't know what he was looking for.

'I really dunno what I'm looking for, Ted. Want to come down and help out?'

Ted held his palms up.

'No way! I'd best stay here and man the doors in case someone tries to get out of the club and spots you.'

'That will be right.'

'Anyway,' said Ted. 'I reckon the first thing you wanna do is pull his head in from the high street in case …'

Which was the exact moment when a joyrider driven SUV skidded up onto the pavement outside La Salsa and flattened Richard's head like a pancake.

STOP THAT GIRL

'Not bad, Be-Bop,' said Tony. 'Not bad, but not great.'

They were in one of Mad Tony Cook's many offices. This was a cramped broom closet above Curl up N Di, the hairdresser's shop owned by his niece, Diane. Tony was wearing a double-breasted pin stripe suit. He had his hair slicked back and had drawn on a pencil moustache. They were watching the playback of Binky knocking the shit out of Scopey.

'Looks like the biz to me,' said Be-Bop.

He opened a can of orange Tango.

'Aye, a couple of years ago it would have been a ratings winner,' said Tony. He looked at Be-Bop over his half-moon glasses. 'But *Bar Wars* is old news now. Especially since the scandal died down. And we've got competitors to boot.' He grins at his own joke.

Be-Bop knew that Tony was right, though.

At the start, *Bar Wars* had been a runaway success. The highest rated cable telly show on the box. The demand for watching people kicking the shit out of each other in grubby pubs was surprisingly high. It was easy to get contestants too – drug addicts, alkies, prozzies. Midgets. Pensioners.

And when the Daily Mail ran a shock/outrage story, saying we were 'exploiting the week and the vulnerable in society,' well, ratings went through the roof. But, like all good ideas, *Bar Wars* was ripped off. Copied. There was even talk of a *Celebrity Bar Wars* with George Galloway and Charlie Sheen.

'So, got a plan?' said Be-Bop.

'Of course,' said Tony. 'Nietzsche said that a man without a plan is not a man.'

'Yeah, but he was as batty as a cave full of Guano, so what did he know,' said Be-Bop.

***

A shadow of gloom hung over Father Tim Cook as he watched the slivers of early morning sunlight slice through the stained glass windows of St Martins' church. The church felt cold and cavernous to him these days. His footsteps echoed as he paced the damp floor.

He sighed and realised he'd been doing that a lot lately. Reminded him of his mother. He shivered and looked at his Rolex. It was almost opening time at The Golden Fleece.

Father Tim left the church and took a short-cut across the park, avoiding the attentions of the drug dealers, drunks and prostitutes that congregated there, even at this time of day. He was almost at the rusty wrought-iron gate that led to the high street when a dishevelled, shambling figure stumbled from out of the bushes. He was tall, gangling. Dressed in what had once been an expensive suit but was now tattered and torn. Covered with dirt and excrement. Another city boy down on his luck, maybe. A twat for sure. The pallid skin and glaring red eyes gave him the appearance of a vampire on the prowl.

He reached out a bony hand.

'Spare a …'

Before he could finish his sentence, Tim punched him in the throat and guts. The junkie barely screamed as he stumbled to the ground.

Tim glanced around but no one had noticed. These days, no one had any interest in what happened to a drug addict in a city that was infested with them. Tim dragged the unconscious junky into bushes and headed across the street and into The Golden Fleece.

'The usual, Father,' said Niall, the Golden Fleece's wiry and obtuse barman, who had the annoying habit of never looking anyone in the eye.

Tim nodded.

Niall poured a pint of Stella Artois and placed it on the sticky bar. Tim sat at the corner of the bar watching an old black and white television that was showing a cricket match that seemed to have been dragging on for an eternity.

Niall usually refused to allow a television in his pub but today was a cricket tournament that he felt he just couldn't miss. Tim had no interest in sport, especially cricket, and was almost catatonic. Apart from Tim, the rest of the customers in the pub were weathered and weary old men that were gathered around the bar watching the match like gargoyles at the front of Notre Dame Cathedral.

'This must be what purgatory is like,' said Tim.

'Eh?' said Niall.

'Nothing,' said Tim.

The multi-coloured lanterns that adorned the bar area and the dingy pub's few tables flickered as the front door opened. A tall blonde in a fake leopard-skin coat walked in. She grinned.

'Father Cook,' she said. 'Just the bloke I've been looking for.'

Magda grasped Cook's hand and shook it vigorously. An old, overtly masculine habit from the days when she was known as Marek.

'Let's grab a table,' she said. 'I have some info that'll blow your cobblers off.'

Although Marek had learned a little English whilst serving in the Polish army, Magda's far from sentimental education came from hanging around Liverpool bars just as classy as The Golden Fleece, and even less sophisticated establishments.

They took a seat in a dark corner of the room, beside a broken quiz machine. The small table was illuminated by a shimmering red lantern. Magda took off her coat. She was wearing a sparkly black dress. Her fingernails and lipstick were blood red.

She put her black leather handbag on the table. Groans of disappointment emanated from the bar area.

'What are they watching?' she said.

'Paint stay wet,' said Tim.

Magda rummaged in her bag. She placed a few items on the table: a knuckle-duster, a small gun, a lipstick. And then she took out a Samsung Galaxy S4.

'Have you heard of the motivational guru Nathan North?'

'I have heard of him. There are billboards about the city for his Wembley Arena show/ performance or whatever they call it but who exactly is he?'

'It's an everyday kind of story. Nathan North was once a television chat show host. He was kidnapped while recording a TV programme in Colombia and had some sort of mystical revelation. He eventually set up a series of self-help courses 'The North Method.' And sold books and films of course.'

'Looks like he's doing well for himself'.

'Hold on. There,' she handed Cook her smartphone. 'Have a gander at that while I go and get a drink. Want one?'

Tim looked at his watch.

'Yeah, why not.'

Tim tapped the smartphone screen and a small promotional film appeared. A load of blah blah blah about empowerment and the like. North was a real smarm-bag but if it made him the dosh, Tim couldn't fault him.

Magda sat down as the film was ending.

'Fascinating stuff I'm sure but …'

'You missed it didn't you?' said Magda. She took a big slurp of her Guinness. 'Rewind.'

Tim handed the phone back to her.

'Here, you do it. I hate using other people's phones.'

Magda tapped the screen and froze it at the point she was look for.

'There,' she said, and showed the picture to Tim. Nathan North was shaking hands with a weedy man who looked like a vampire.

'You want to find Ron Moody, there you are.'

He handed the phone back to Magda.

'Well spotted, Maggie May. A nice little bonus will be coming your way.'

***

Stephanie Harvey had the bluest eyes that Scrace had ever seen and they seemed to twinkle non-stop, reminding her of the stars in the night sky when she had a joint. She could almost feel herself floating into them. Drowning. She smiled but Harvey's cold, hard expression never changed.

Harvey stood in the corner of the interview in a suit so sharp she could use it to shave her legs. She flamboyantly took off her milky white Stetson and started wagging a finger again.

'But then, most people are predictable, truth be told. They just can't see outside the limits of their own experience. Can't think outside the box, they have a paucity of imagination. Which is why it occurs to me, Ms Scrace, that perhaps you and your estimable colleagues are not treating my client's predicament with the due amount of seriousness,' she said.

Harvey had the sort of yawning Southern drawl that Scrace had only ever heard in American films and she did wonder for a moment whether she was putting it on and was actually from Barnsley or Cleethorpes.

'And I can assure you, Ms Harvey, that we are according your client's case the amount of seriousness that it merits. And that's Detective Inspector Scrace to you, thank you very much.' She glanced at her smartphone but there was still nothing from Ronnie about the errant fences Aldo Calcagno and Ron Moody.

'Then could you please inform me as to how your investigations are progressing?' said Harvey. She turned a chair back to front and sat on it, facing DI Scrace.

'Well, although we have nothing concrete,' said Scrace. 'A little later this afternoon we'll be meeting a very successful fence who specialises in the buying and selling of more exotic items. If anyone is going to try and move your client's comics, they are sure to contact him.'

Scrace tapped the wooden table.

'Let's hope you do. From what I understand your department does not need any further bad publicity. Not since the incident with your predecessor.'

Scrace squirmed. One of her former colleagues had been found dead in a Moroccan bordello with enough dope in him to fly to the moon and a red high-heeled shoe stuck up his jacksy. The tabloids had a field day, of course.

'A new broom has swept this department clean, Ms Harvey. It is now spic and span.'

Harvey looked around the grubby room, a look of distaste on her face.

'Not literally, of course,' said Scrace.

Harvey cracked a smile. Reached into her jacket pocket and took a pack of red Marlborough.

'I'm guessin' I not allowed to smoke around here,' she said.

'Good God no,' said Scrace. 'That's a hanging offense these days.'

'I'd heard you Europeans were less hung up on the health Nazism.'

'Yeah, once upon a time. But these days everything is becoming more and more homogenised. You can't even smoke in a French café!'

'That is shocking. Next thing you'll be telling me they have civilised rest rooms.'

'Oh, I'm sure the toilets are of the same low hygienic standards.'

Harvey got up. 'Want to join me?'

'Well, I've been three months free of the cancer sticks but one can't hurt, eh?' she said, tasting the nicotine and almost salivating.

***

Rossiter didn't think he'd heard anyone scream so much and so hysterically. Especially a grown man.

'Get them out of here! Get them out of here!' screamed Cane, pulling off his Batman mask, and wrapping himself with one of the bedroom's thick, red velvet curtains.

Rossiter sighed and picked up the butterfly net that he'd found in one of mansion's many rooms. With a couple of scoops he'd caught the two bats that were giving The Dark Knight such consternation, opened the window they come in from and threw them out.

'Rossiter, you mention this to anyone and you are dead! Clear?' said Cane.

'Crystal,' said Rossiter.

Cane unravelled himself from the curtain and unsteadily got down from the table he'd been stood on. He picked up a decanter of expensive brandy and swigged it. Started coughing.

'This goddamn country,' he yelled, spraying Rossiter with Cognac.

'Indeed,' said Rossiter, wiping himself with a napkin. 'Such a barbaric place.'

***

'How many other people do you know who have Tricky Dicky tattooed around their neck,' said Squeaky. He dropped Richard's body back onto the office floor.

Marty groaned inwardly and poured himself a brandy. Hoped the corpse wouldn't stain the carpet. He'd been a fair bit peeved when he thought the kid he'd dumped in the wheelie bin earlier had croaked but now he was more even pissed off. And worried.

'What I want to know is how my half- brother ended up in a wheelie bin at the back of La Salsa with his head caved in? And who did this to him?' said Marty.

It wasn't as if Marty actually liked Richard Sanderson. In fact, he'd hated the twat. The whole blue-eyed boy prodigal son shtick had grated on him from the very beginning. But family was family and who knew what his dad and Uncle Tony would say.

Squeaky opened up a packet of salted peanuts and tucked in.

'And what happened to that other kid? The Baghead?' he said.

'Now, that is the he least of our worries,' said Marty. 'If Dad or Uncle Tony thinks we had anything to do with this there'll be all manner of shit storms coming our way. And not enough umbrellas.'

'So, what's the story?'

'Just dump him. Somewhere out of town,' said Marty.

'Jed Bramble's farm? Them pigs'll scoff anything.'

***

Scopey's Scooby Doo voice had lost a lot of its earlier gusto. He had taken the Stanley knife and shakily slid it across the palm of his left hand. Screamed. Binky offered him a bottle of whisky and a bandage. Scopey dropped the knife and knocked the booze back as he held his blood-stained hand to the camera.

'Careful you don't stain the desk,' said Tony. 'Teak, that is.'

Tony's new venture was really taking off. Live Videocams. Not the tired old stripping housewives, though. The deal was that punters paid to watch the likes of Scopey hurt himself. The more they paid, the more he sliced himself up.

An Austrian had even offered a small fortune if Scopey cut off a finger. Or two. Or more. So far, Scopey had agreed to everything but who knew how far he'd go. The choice was his, of course.

For some reason, it reminded Be-Bop of that old telly series, *The Twilight Zone*, and the presenter who said that our only limits were our imagination. He wasn't far wrong. Be-Bop's mobile buzzed. A text message from Tim Cook and he was happy to receive it.

***

Turban Ted had soon scarpered after Richard Sanderson's head had been splattered, and Kenny had been forced to drag the corpse into the alleyway at the back of the club. Then he'd managed to haul Richard's body into a wheelie bin until the end of his shift. Luckily it was pouring with rain and the high street was pretty much deserted so no one had spotted him but it had been a close thing a couple of times. He'd taken a bucket of bleach and scrubbed away what was left of Richard's noggin but it seemed to leave a green stain that really did look like the shape of a head.

There had been a head wrecker of a few hours but after the club closed up he went out into the pouring rain, collar of his leather jacket turned up, and head into the alleyway. As he went over to the wheelie bin a white Audi turned the corner.

'Turban Ted to the rescue,' shouted Ted.

'Well, covering your own arse, more like it,' said Kenny.

Ted pulled on a bright yellow cagoule and got out of the car.

'Who's that?' said Ted, nodding toward the corpse that Kenny was dragging from the wheelie-bin.

'Eh,' said Kenny. 'You know who it is. It Richard bleeding Sanderson. He's …'

He gasped for breath as he laid the corpse on the rain-soaked ground.

'I know who it isn't,' said Ted. 'Look.'

He took out a small torch that was attached to a key ring and shined it in Baghead Berry's face.

'Bugger,' said Kenny. 'That's not Richard Sanderson.'

'No shit Sherlock.'

Kenny looked over at the two wheelie bins that were at the rear of La Salsa.

'How the f ...'

'And I'll tell you something else for nothing,' said Ted, poking Baghead. 'He's not brown bread, either.'

NOBODY'S SCARED

Noola's Saloon was even more crowded than the pub they'd just left but that certainly didn't deter Father Tim and Gregor, who had decided they were on a drinking mission. As they shuffled through the door, the Wurlitzer jukebox burst to life and Howling Wolf snarled out 'I Ain't Superstitious.'

The pub was dimly lit and smoky, despite the fact that no one was smoking. Gregor found a small table near a disused cigarette machine and Tim went to the bar. A dishevelled and unshaven old soak, who seemed to be dressed like a private eye from some old black and white film, nestled on a bar stool, calmly contemplating the glass of whisky that was in front of him. The ice cubes seemed to shimmer, glimmer and glow in the wan light.

He looked up at Tim.

'Twilight time,' he said, his hangdog expression never changing.

'Isn't it always,' said Tim.

The old soak nodded and went back to staring at his drink.

Tim briefly turned his gaze outside. The wet pavement reflected Noola's Saloon's flickering neon sign. Headlights cut through the heavy rain. He unsteadily shuffled up and leaned on the bar, plonking the sleeve of his jacket in a puddle of spilt lager.

After a while, he caught the eye of the barman, a grumpy-looking bloke with a pock-marked face and inky black quiff. He slowly put down his copy of National Geographic and Tim made the two finger gesture for two pints, making sure his hand was facing the right way.

The antique Wurlitzer Jukebox was playing Mel Torme's version of *Gloomy Sunday*. Tim had always been a big fan of The Velvet Fog but the cacophonous voice of a fat bald bloke in a corduroy jacket boomed over the lush sounds.

'Well, I'm certainly not a fan of the popcorn trash that the multiplex inflict upon us but at least Christopher Nolan treats Batman with the gravitas he deserves,' said a bald, fat man.

A tall, twitchy man who was looming over him almost spat his half pint of Guinness over his Armani shirt.

'Gravitas!? It's about a bloke who dresses up in a rubber bat suit to fight a baddy who dresses up like a clown. It's not exactly Marcel bloody Proust, is it?'

'Well some critics would argue that it's a metaphor for ...'

'Critics! Jeez! Film critics! Have you ever been to the BFI?'

'Of course. The recent Alain Resnais retrospective was ...'

'The British Film Institute is a very creepy place, indeed, my friend. Creepy people, too. And the shite they spout. Like that crap about *Dawn of The Dead* being a satire of consumerism because the zombies go to a shopping centre. I mean, that's one gag in the whole film! There's also a scene where one of them gets decapitated by a helicopter blade. Is it a satire of air traffic control? Eh? I ask you?'

The bald man shuffled in his seat and wiped cappuccino froth from his top lip.

'Well ...'

Father Tim, picked up two pints of Kronenburg from the bar and resisted the temptation to give both of the blokes a slap.

'Wankers like that are what put me off going out for a drink in the west end these days,' he said as he put the drinks on the table.

'The city is riddled with them these days,' said Gregor. 'They're like the clap. Even worse than northerners.'

'I was in that poncy over-priced sandwich shop before I came here,' said Tim, unsteadily sitting down. 'Away in a Manger or whatever it's called. Anyway, they were playing Nick Drake. *Fruit Tree* to be precise.'

'I like Nick Drake,' said Gregor.

'Now, don't get me wrong, I like a bit of Nick myself but there were a couple of media wankers in there talking about his mum's LP'

'Whose mum?'

'Nick Drake. Some sad bastard has put out a few songs she record in the olden days.'

'Any good?'

'Dunno. Never heard it. Anyway, these twats in the sandwich shop started prattling on about how Drake and his mother's music was 'quintessentially English'. I mean what the fuck's that all about? Quintessentially posh sissy boy with a quintessentially stuck-up mother, I'll give you that. Quintessentially poncy. It's all that John Betjeman, cricket on the village green, *Downtown Abbey*, Latin quoting detective cobblers that they punt to the septics because, well, yanks are thick. And it has nothing to do with the life of a hairdresser from Wolverhampton or a bingo caller from Hull or the vast majority of English people. You know what I'm saying?'

'Poshness. Poshnessabounds,' slurred Gregor, sinking even lower in his seat. 'This country is crippled by its class system.'

'Exactly. Switch on the telly and it's all Sherlock poncy Holmes or Dr poncy Who. This is the bullshit we have to put up with. Oxbridge twots and Oxbridge wannabees.'

'We need another class war, that is what we need,' said Gregor. He spilt a splash of lager on his shirt as he slurped it.

'I blame America for it … well, I blame America for everything …The United States of America is a cancer. A poisonous virus that has fatally infected its host,' said Tim, reclining in the leather chair and waggling his outstretched fingers, trying to get the circulation back in them. He checked his reflection in the mirror. He wasn't looking so good.

'It's like in those horror films, eh?' he said. 'They say you shouldn't make your home on an Indian burial ground but when you think about it, the whole of the United States is a bleedin Indian burial ground. Think about it.'

'I had a lovely time in that Florida, mind you,' said Bev the manicurist, who had come back from the toilets and sat down next to them. She was a leathery Kunta Kinti blonde with a permanent Joker grin due to plastic surgery that went pear shaped. She worked at Curl up N Di, the hairdressers owned by Tony Cook's niece, Diana.

Tim ignored her. Her botched Botox grated on him.

'They don't even have their own language let alone sports,' continued Tim. 'I mean, they play rounders – a girls' game and look what they've done to rugby? It's a disgrace! The player's wearing crash helmets and padded cushion. Big Jessies.'

'It's political correctness gone mad, is what it is,' said Bev. 'Treating grown men like babies.'

'And then there's the two world wars. They wait until the end, until everyone's knackered and then they swan in claiming they won the bleedin thing. That's just cheating, that is. '

'My Tariq always does that when I try to open a bottle of brown sauce,' said Bev. 'He waits till I've loosened it and …Oh, bugger. Here's that Geordie bloke that works for your Uncle Tony. I'll come back later. I can't understand a bloody word he says and it gets right on my nips.'

She knocked back her gin and tonic. Crunched the ice.

'I think you'll find that Be-Bop DeLuca isn't a Geordie. He's a Mackam or a Sanddancer or maybe a Smoggie. Could even be a Monkey Hanger,' said Tim.

'What's the difference, then? They're all barbaric northern scum as far as I'm concerned,' smiled Bev.

'Who exactly is Be-Bop?' said Gregor.

'Be-Bop DeLuca,' said Tim, 'Is a saxophone player and hired muscle who once worked for Captain Cutlass, one of the north east's biggest villains. Heard of him?'

'Can't say I have.'

'He used to have a habit of waving a sword around although I think the actual sword in question was a rapier. Anyway, when Cutlass went boring and legit Be-Bop upped sticks and moved down here to work for Uncle Tony for a bit. He plays regular Sunday afternoon gigs in a boozer over Earl's Court.'

'Well, I'll be off for a bit,' said Bev. She blew Be-Bop a kiss as she left the pub.

'My round is it?' said Be-Bop, taking off his beret and Crombie, and leaning his saxophone case against the jukebox.

'My Lord, a northerner getting the drinks in,' Tim crossed himself. 'I can't turn down that opportunity,' he said.

While they waited for Be-Bop to come back with the drinks, Tim continued his rant, including Stephen Fry, Emma Thompson, the Home Counties, and shops with too many varieties of pasta. Gregor nodded off.

'Dearest the shadows I live with are numberless,' sang Be-Bop, gruffly singing along to the Mel Torme song that was playing.

He placed the drinks on the table. Tim gave Gregor a shove and woke him up.

'So, what's the SP on this Nathan North twot?' said Tim.

'He's minted for sure. Married to some sit-com actress. Dolly bird I've never heard of. No kids. He's got a big fancy pad over in Chiswick,' said Be-Bop. 'Hangs around the usually shite Soho joints; The French House, Groucho. Wankers Unanimous.'

'What about locally?' said Tim

'He drinks in a pub called The Tabard. Know it?'

'Can't say I do,' said Tim.

'I do,' said Gregor. 'It has a small repertory theatre above it. I've been there a couple of times. They did a great production of Pinter's *Dumb Waiter*.'

'Not too fond of Pinter,' said Be-Bop. 'I'm more of a Samuel Becket man.'

'I like a pinter lager myself,' said Tim.

The others groaned.

Tim ignored them and took out his smartphone. Phoned Bev.

'Bev, get your juicy arse back here pronto. You're going west young woman.'

***

The silence dragged like a BNP voter's knuckles and Niki Scrace felt as if she were going to explode but the nutter just kept on staring at her, occasionally waving around the knife in his hand. His left eye twitching. The hand with the knife wobbling.

She'd made the silly mistake of taking a short cut through a darkened alleyway on the way home, after having a couple of pints in the pub. And of course she'd stumbled into a mugging. The twitchy nutter had his knife to the throat of an old piss head that was dressed like Sam Spade – pin stripe suit, trench coat, trilby – the lot.

Scrace had taken out her nightstick and walked up behind the crim but had slipped on a discarded kebab. The nutter turned and the old soak ran off.

She slowly got to her feet, noticing that the nightstick had slipped across the floor and was beside an over-spilling wheelie bin.

The nutter was clearly a junkie and could have been aged anywhere between fifteen or fifty. He had an eye tattooed in the middle of his forehead and Scrace eventually realised she knew who he was.

'It's Dean isn't it?' she said.

The nutter squinted at her.

'It is. It's Dean Vincent. From the Aylesbury Estate,' she said.

He looked uncomfortable. Twitched more aggressively.

'Yeah, I might be, but who are you?' he said.

Niki supressed a grin as she stepped toward him.

'Don't you remember me, Dean?'

He squinted so much it was like his eyes had disappeared into his head.

'Never seen you before in my life?' he said.

'Yes, you have Dean. In fact, the last time you saw me you were ripping off punters down cruisers creek. Offered me your arse you did and then tried to rip me off, too. I broke your little finger as I remember.'

The nutter looked as if the world was spinning on its axis.

'You must remember your old mate DS Jimmy Scrace.'

She pushed her face in front of Dean and grinned. Dean's own face was slowly transformed into a look of horror, anguish.

'No … No … No …'he said.

He turned and ran, dropping the knife behind him. Scrace was too busy laughing to give chase. She reckoned Dean's DT's were going to be a lot worse than usual tonight.

***

A hairy Matt Cane howled as he leapt from the dome of the Basilica and onto the roof of the old theatre. His shape silhouetted against the full moon and he howled again. One more jump and he smashed through the windows of the Inter-Euro Hotel, crashing into the four poster bed where Dolph Lundgren with a buzz cut and a swastika tattoo humped a blow up doll dressed in military uniform.

As Cane leapt, the Austrian swung a machete at the wolfman's shoulder.

The television screen went red.

Rossiter couldn't help it, he clapped. Furiously.

'Oh, this really is marvellous fun, Mr Cane,' he said.

And it was. For years he'd had to endure sitting through private screenings of Cane films. Lumpen action movies or even worse turgid dramas about prodigal sons bonding with absentee fathers – Matt Cane seemed to make a lot of that schlock.

But this new series for the cable television channel HBO was very good stuff indeed. Admittedly, Cane didn't have to do a great deal of acting in the show, and a stuntman did all of the action stuff but the writer and director clearly knew what they were doing.

'Kinda cool, eh?' said Cane. He was sat on the floor, leaning against a black leather sofa, drinking Evian from the bottle. Rossiter reclined in a large leather armchair, drinking Cognac.

'If the viewing public have any taste at all, 'Roman Dalton – *Werewolf PI*' will be a smash hit. Please pass on my congratulations to Mr Rodriguez the next time you see him.'

'Will do. The show kicks ass for sure. A lot better than that last TV show I did.'

'Ah, *The Jazz Detective*. Yes, after reading one or two of Ms Peters' books I was sure that particular programme wouldn't be your style.' And Rossiter remembered that Cane's Welsh accent was particularly painful. Even more painful than a genuine Welsh accent. Which was saying something.

Cane stood up and stretched. Went over to the table and picked up his smartphone

'God-damn! Still nothing from Harvey. What the hell is that carpet muncher up to?'

'I'm sure Ms Harvey is on the trail of the errant com … er, sequential art as we speak,' said Rossiter, hastily topping up his Cognac. He could see Cane's temper bubbling to boiling point. 'You wouldn't happen to have the next episode of *Werewolf PI*. Would you?'

Cane cooled down immediately, a smirk on his face.

'Damn right I do.'

He took a CD from a stainless steel suitcase, put it in the CD player and plonked himself in front of the sofa. Clicked the remote control.

Rossiter leaned close to the TV screen. Matt Cane – now human – stood over a corpse in a dump of a flat.

The coffee table in the flat was littered with empty beer cans; the battered old fridge in the corner made a high pitched whirring sound; the Bakelite radio was smashed over the threadbare carpet; there was a mountain of paperbacks on the wicker rocking chair; dirty laundry was strewn around the place and a stained and ragged paisley blanket was dangling over one of the arms of the brown corduroy sofa.

The corpse, however, was immaculately turned out. Apart from the machete in his chest. And the patch of blood that had spread across the front of his pink Hugo Boss shirt. And the shape of a pentangle that had been burned into his neck.

Rossiter shifted in his seat. Enthralled.

And then the doorbell rang.

***

'Cobblers!' said Squeaky.

He'd been trying for about ten minutes to park the massive Actros Titan truck in the alleyway at the back of La Salsa but it was just too bloody big.

'Bollocks!' said Marty, who was stood in the doorway of the club, hands gripping his hips. He took a deep breath, gestured for Squeaky to get out of the cabin and went back inside.

Squeaky wheezed up the steps behind him.

'No good, boss,' he gasped.

Marty nodded wearily. He walked behind the bar and poured a pint of Carling. Handed it to Squeaky.

'Ta much, boss.' Squeaky knocked it back in one. Wiped the froth from his mouth.

'We're going to have to get him out through the front door, so try to park as close as you can,' said Marty, pouring himself a pint of Stella.

'Okey dokey, boss,' said Squeaky.

'And make sure you park that thing as far away from here as possible before you torch it. The last thing we want is dad and Uncle Tony making a connection with us.'

'I spoke to Jed Bramble,' said Squeaky. 'He reckons he can do away with your Richard no bother.'

'Yeah, I've been thinking about Jed. Good idea but that means going out of London. It's a long way to pig shagging land. If you get stopped by the filth, none of them coppers are likely to be our boys.'

'Well, there's a shitty bit of waste land over South East London,' said Squeaky.

'The whole of South East London is a shitty bit of waste land, Squeaky. You need to be more specific.'

'The Aylesbury Estate. It's near the Elephant & Castle. There's been all sorts of riots and shit going on lately. After the filth did a drug raid on the wrong house and knocked ten buckets of shite out of a priest or other,' said Squeaky.

He popped a breath mint into his mouth.

'Sounds like the perfect place to me,' said Marty, loosening his tie. 'You want someone to go with you?'

'Naw, I'll do it on me todd, like,' said Squeaky.

Marty looked at him puzzled.

'On me own.'

'Okay,' said Marty. 'As long as you don't need an interpreter. They've got inside toilets up there.'

***

Kenny couldn't believe it, but there it was. His truck. The Actros Titan. The one that had been nicked was now heading up the high street, away from La Salsa.

'Go on, put your foot down,' he said. 'Don't let that thieving bastard get away.'

Ted made a 'harrumph' sound and drove off, glancing in the mirror at the Ratboy in the back seat, who seemed to be coming around.

'Hit him again,' he said.

Kenny leaned over from the passenger seat and whacked the skinny youth with a sock full of coins. It seemed to do the trick.

Ted switched on the radio and Robbie William's *Angels* wafted through the air as the car headed into the Aylesbury Estate. The place was already lit up with joy riders torching the cars they'd stolen earlier. A fish and chip shop looked as if it had only just been fire-bombed. Rockets filled the sky.

'It sorta kinda looks beautiful,' said Ted.

Kenny ignored him. He was squinting as he peered into the darkness, looking for the truck.

'You know, this is the most performed song in Karaoke these days,' said Ted, turning up the music. He started singing along.

Kenny grimaced and turned off the music.

'Pay attention, won't you. This is my livelihood here.'

Ted sulked and looked out of the window as he headed deeper into the estate.

'By the way, remember The Sniffler?' said Ted.

'I don't think so. What is it a horror film?'

Ted laughed.

'Naw, short-arsed geezer. He used to be a regular in The Blue Anchor most weekdays. Had big, bushy eyebrows that looked like caterpillars. He drank tonic water and kept stuffing a Vick's Inhaler up his nose, in between sniffs.'

'Ah, yeah. I remember him. He hasn't been in there for quite a while, I think.'

'Too right. Well, that there was a bloke with a story, I can tell you. Turns out he used to be an accountant for some big import/export firm that went bankrupt. Seems he didn't have the heart to tell his wife he was out of a job so he used to leave home every day as if he was going to work and he spent most of his time in the library or here.'

'Mm. Well, I doubt he could keep up that pretence for too long and then his money would presumably run out. Or his wife would find out.'

'Ah, well, that was what happened, you see. One day he left his mobile phone at home and his missus found it and rang his firm to tell him that he'd forgotten it. But they told her he didn't work there no more.'

'Ah.'

'And then it gets weirder. She started nosing about in his phone and found a shit load of women's phone numbers. She checks into them and finds out they all belong to call girls. Puts two and two together and makes 69. Thinks that's where he's been spending his days. Then she checks the bank statements to see how much he's been spending on the ladies. And the big surprise is that money hasn't been going out it's been coming in.'

'Curious.'

'Anyway, turns out that our mate The Sniffler was approached by a young, professional lady one day and turned down her advances but after a chinwag with her decided to go into the 'madam' business himself. He's doing quite well too, targeting his old business contacts and the like.'

'Good luck to him,' said Kenny.

They drove in silence listening to an eighties radio station. China Crisis, Johnny Hates Jazz, and *Wonderful Life* by Black. As they pulled into The Aylesbury Estate Kenny was almost drifting off.

And then his heart started beating in a weird jazz rhythm.

'Bingo!' he said. 'There it is.'

The truck was in the car park of what used to be The Blue Anchor pub before it had been gutted in an arson attack. Shattered glass sparkled like stars. A fat bloke stood beside it with two cans of petrol in his hands.

'Right, let's get that fat fucker,' said, Kenny.

'Who is he?'

'No idea.'

'What if he's tooled up?' said Ted.

'Well, he won't be the only one,' said Kenny, patting the Glock he had in his pocket.

Looked like his instincts were right.

'Fair do's,' said Ted. 'But maybe we should get some reinforcements'.

WHAT'S THE MATTER BOY?

The metallic evening had gasped for life until it was smothered by the night as Father Tim Cook pulled into the caravan site and parked beside Booze N News. He locked up his bike.

He went into the shop and went to the fridge for a can of orange Tango. A super tall Sikh with a goatee stood behind the counter eating a Christmas Dinner Flavoured Pot Noodle.

'Mornin,' he said, in a strong Birmingham accent.

'Looks like it is,' said Tim.

'Seasonal carry-ons catching up with you?' said the Sikh.

'You could say that,' said Tim.

He looked out of the window.

'Which one of them caravans is Ron Moody's?' he said.

The Sikh snorted.

'Why not hazard a guess?' he said.

All the caravans were pretty much identical, painted cream of off-white. All except one which was painted red with a black death's head on the side and had a flapping pirate flag flying above it.

'Aye, it wasn't exactly Mastermind stuff, was it? Is he in?'

'He hardly ever goes out these days. Sometimes pops in here for few cans of Special Brew. His crew visit from time to time. Bring him his supplies. Are you a mate of his, like?'

'I knew him well enough. Once upon a time,' said Tim.

He paid for the drink, opened it and knocked it back. Burped.

'Ta much,' he said.

He walked over to the caravan and knocked on its metal door. Nothing. He knocked again, harder this time, but there was still no sound.

He noticed that the door was ajar and eased it open with a creak.

'Ron, it's me. Father Tim. I've got a package for you from Uncle Tony'

Nothing. So Tim stepped inside.

The caravan was old and creaky and a nasty, fusty smell hit you as soon as you stepped in. There was a plasma television showing a documentary about the World Trade Centre and a small fridge, that looked like the ones you found in hotel rooms, hummed. It had a small transistor radio plonked on the top that leaked out an Elton John song about Marilyn Monroe. A round coffee table and a couple of kitchen chairs were next to the grubby window. There was a pyramid of beer cans on the table. A mountain of ash in a glass ashtray. The walls were adorned with flags – the union jack, a swastika, the Weimar Republic, Argentina. And there was a bed. Which was where Ron Moody lay, smothered in blankets and looking more than somewhat dead.

Father Tim Cook paused for a moment to catch his breath, before soaking the fence's body with the remains of a bottle of cheap supermarket vodka and half a bottle of Gordon's gin. As an old advertising jingle corkscrewed through his thoughts, Tim struck a match and threw it onto the corpse. He waited for it to catch light and then carefully closed the front door and walked out into the cold, granite day, his breath trapped tight within his chest.

He put in his head phones and clicked on his smartphone. Martin Stephenson sang about a 'Little Red Bottle' and he started to wind down. The Aylesbury Estate was alight. Sirens screamed. There were explosions. Shouts. Dogs barking. This was London. His London.

Tim remembered that there used to be a half-decent boozer nearby. The Ancient Oak had gained a bit of a reputation since it was one of the first locals to offer striptease shows afterhours. Some of the dancers threw in a bit extra, too. Maybe a hand shandy would lighten his load.

The last few weeks had been a bit of a twatter. Teetering on the cusp of a debacle. Especially hunting down Ron Moody. Bev had gone to The Tabard pub and had tried to pick up Nathan North but later found out that he was good with colours, and was knocking off a local copper. Then Lisa, North's missus, turned up and tried it on with Bev.

Bev was, apparently 'in a horny dilemma.' In the end she went back with Lisa gave her a good tongue lashing and found out where Ron Moody was staying to boot.

And so business was done. But Father Tim had been getting these twinges. He wouldn't have called it a guilty conscience but there was something – more like a noose- pulling at him. He'd even started to have dreams, for the first time in his life. Nightmares. He'd always considered that to be the sign of weak character. Unfulfilled lives.

As he approached The Ancient Oak, time saw that it was boarded up, stained with graffiti. And then he heard voices. There was a massive truck parked on a piece of waste ground and a small group of men were yelling at each other. A small bonfire nearby lit up their faces and Tim was sure he recognised at least one of them. He approached carefully, a hand on the gun in his pocket.

'Alright Father,' said one of the Ratboys.

As he got close to the graffiti stained tower blocks, he was starting to sober up and the hangover was biting. It wasn't a particularly good feeling. He strongly felt the need for a drink. He noticed that the bar in The Ancient Oak was lit up, the sounds of Suzi Quatro's *Can the Can* bursting from inside so he crossed the street.

The Ancient Oak, like a fair amount of its clientele, was all fur coat and no knickers. It had lived up to its name once upon a time and its facade was still pretty impressive but the interior, however, left a lot to be desired. For many years, it had survived as a nightclub which was just about bog standard, with the emphasis on the bog.

Every Thursday, it was 'Super Seventies Special' because, unsurprisingly, the music that was played was from the seventies and all drinks were 70p. Unfortunately, most of the clientele were knocking on seventy, too, which is why it had the earned its reputation as a 'grab a granny night.'

Tim walked inside. The pub was crowded, hot and clammy. Billy Blockbuster, the DJ and quizmaster, was playing smoochy songs back-to-back. As *Betcha By Golly Wow* played, a mountain of a man drunkenly canoodled with a couple of members of the cast of *The Golden Girls*. He could hardly stand up, and the pensioners were doing all that they could to support him, but it wouldn't be long before Goliath would crash down. And, before you could shout 'Timber!' he was over, crushing one of the women beneath him. Two identical bouncers in Crombie overcoats, Darren and Dane Greenwood, ran over and hauled him to his feet. They escorted him to the front door with a struggle.

Tim used the distraction to sneak to the front of the bar and catch the eye of the barmaid. She was a tall blonde with sparkling blue eyes and a 1000-watt smile.

'What can I get you, please?' she said in an Eastern European accent sharp enough to shave with.

'Pint of Guinness, please,' said Tim.

She poured it with a struggle and frowned as she attempted to draw a shamrock on the head. The other customers shouted for her to get a move on but she seemed oblivious, lost in concentration.

'Sorry,' she said, as she put it on the bar in front of me. 'It's not so easy.'

'Now worries,' said Tim. 'I'll have a JD chaser, too.'

'A what?'

'Jack Daniels. Whisky.'

She turned to the optics behind the bar and stared at them as if they were a magic eye picture.

'Any whisky will do,' he shouted. 'I really don't mind.'

Eventually she found a bottle of Glenfidich. She poured it carefully, turned and put the drink on the bar.

'First night here?' said Tim.

'My first night working in a bar,' she said. 'My friend was sick and asked me to ... represent her.'

Tim looked at the baying crowd that had gathered at the bar.

'You'd best serve some of The Walking Dead there,' he said. 'They're looking bloodthirsty.'

She smiled and served an aging teddy boy with a tattooed face that looked as if it was melting.

Tim turned around and leaned against the bar. The music changed from Steve Harley's *Come Up And See Me* to The Stranglers' *Something Better Change* and he started to relax for the first time in days. Some things had changed, no doubt about it

The barmaid would have stood out like a sore thumb when he was growing up. More than a few of the faces where familiar, though and he tried to piece together what he knew about them. The ageing teddy boy was The Dummy. He'd been born mute and was unable to speak until he was well into his twenties. The nick name stuck, of course. Spit The Dog stood at the corner of the bar, sipping a bottle of Becks and occasionally spitting into a plastic bottle. Due to a glandular problem, as Tim remembered. Spit was dressed in denim, his long ginger hair going thin on top. His mother had won the football pools when he was a teenager and he'd inherited a decent amount when she'd died of an accidental drug overdose. He seemed to be pissing most of that fortune away by the looks of things. There were worse ways to die.

Tim finished both of his drinks and contemplated getting more when a Phil Collins song kicked in. he took that as his cue to leave.

***

Niki Scrace knew she was dancing like an idiot. Like a spaced-out teenage fool. But she didn't give a shit. The sense of relief was phenomenal.

'I knew I could have decked him,' she said. 'Not a problem. But I froze.'

The cowboy gnome smiled knowingly.

'Yeah, I was into spinning the knife. Like when I was a kid. Knives never frighten me. They should, I know, though.'

The Batman gnome, who was usually silent, gave a big thumbs up sign.

'But it dragged me by my cobblers into the real world. Made me realise how much I have to live for. Take the bull by the horns.'

'Or the cowgirl,' said Stephanie Harvey, stepping into the garden wearing only a red Kimono and smoking a joint.

***

Rivulets of rain ponderously trailed down the windscreen as Rossiter watched Matt Cane stagger out of the sleazy pub and tumble toward the Mercedes. A truck pulled into the car park and a skinhead in a tartan shirt got out of the truck and rushed into the pub, sending Cane whirling.

Cane opened one of the back doors and staggered into the back seat.

'I've got it, Alfred. Get moving.'

Rossiter started up the car with a deep sigh. He wasn't big on drugs. Legal or illegal. He occasionally partook of the odd puff of wacky backy but that was it. He was always careful not to overindulge, though he had heard that one of the side effects was paranoia. And cocaine caused that for sure. But something had snapped and Cane was now calling him Alfred.

'Faster, Alfred,' said Cane

Rossiter had repeatedly told Cane that his name was Brian but to no avail. He increased his speed.

***

Marty was massaging his head a little too vigorously and it was starting to hurt even more. He couldn't believe what he'd just seen on La Salsa's CCTV playback tapes. His bouncer Kenny Rogan kicking the shit out of his half-brother. What a pillock.

He was contemplating getting pissed and dealing with that particular problem at a later date when his phone rang.

'Mr Cook, is it ready?' said Stephanie Harvey.

'It most certainly is Ms Harvey. You can collect it in the morning.'

'A pleasure doing business with you.'

'Likewise.'

Marty hung up and leaned over to his drinks cabinet. His phone rang again.

He looked at the display. Squeaky.

'Is it done?' he said.

'We've got a problem, boss,' said Squeaky.

A deep sigh.

'What sort of problem.'

'Well it's … oh, bugger!'

Marty jerked the phone away from his ears as he heard gunshot.

***

'Right, you fat twat,' shouted Kenny. 'What do you think you're doing with my truck?'

He was waving the gun around so much and was so angry that he couldn't see where he was walking and tripped over an upturned shopping trolley that someone had been using to barbecue sausages. The gun went off narrowly missing Father Tim as he stepped into the shadows.

'Oh, bugger,' said Squeaky who pulled out a gun and fired at Kenny, narrowly missing him.

'Cobblers!' said Turban Ted.

He ran back to the car as Squeaky waddled over to Kenny who was struggling to stand. Ted pretty swiftly dragged the Ratboy out of his car and got out of there faster than a formula one driver.

Then there was a blood curdling scream.

Matt Cane screamed again as he leapt off the roof of the truck and landed on Squeaky who shot Kenny in the head splattering Cane and Squeaky with blood and guts.

Rossiter arrived in the car as Cane began knocking ten bells out of Squeaky.

'Mr Cane, come on,' he shouted out of the window but Cane ignored him. Rossiter got out of the car.

'Master Bruce, quick!' he shouted and dragged Cane away from Squeaky, who had dropped his gun.

'Hold on, a minute,' said Cane and he smashed Squeaky in the face with a black boomerang.

As Rossiter stuffed Cane into the back of his car, Be-Bop DeLuca arrived in a taxi. Slowly and carefully they got out and surveyed the carnage.

Kenny was as dead as Di and Dodi by the looks of him, and Squeaky was now rolling around on the floor, screaming in agony.

'What's the fuck has been going on here?' said Be-Bop. 'I should have stayed up north.'

The Ratboy had a big bruise and an even bigger grin on his face as he picked up Kenny 's gun, stuffed it into his hoodie pocket and climbed into the truck's cabin. It was a pain to start at first but he managed to get it moving, it only stalled a couple of times. He reckoned the truck was worth a fair whack and he knew exactly who to sell it to. Tony Cook would be most impressed when he showed it to him. Yes he friggin well would.

'What the fuck are we supposed to do now, then?' said Be-Bop.

'Fancy a pint?' said Father Tim, stepping out of the shadows with a grin on his face.

COLD LONDON BLUES

'Dead centre of town,' said the taxi driver when he dropped Marty Cook off outside the cemetery's wrought-iron gates. Marty got out, paid, and walked through the rain towards the grave. It was packed. Half of the gangsters in the town were there to give Kenny Rogan a send-off as well as a couple of coppers, including DI Scrace and DS Burke. Marty Nodded at them. Rogan's wife was shaking, looking like a kid, her arm around Turban Ted, who was actually crying. Tim and Uncle Tony stood under a weeping willow tree taking sips from a hip flask.

Reverend Abbott, his long hair flowing in the cold north wind, began his familiar eulogy.

'There comes a time in every young man's life,' he said, his long arms stretched wide, 'when he knows that he will never be The Fonz. Shortly after that realisation it becomes clear that he won't even be Richie Cunningham. And so, then, he has to make a choice. Will he be Ralph Malph or Potsie Weber? But there are some men...'

Marty tuned out after that. Reverend Abbott's frankly barmy sermons were as famous as his acid flashbacks. It was clear where he was going, though. Kenny was cannon fodder, pure and simple. Always had been.

After Kenny Rogan's funeral, Mary Cook wandered off in a daze. He'd bought his plane ticket and put the house and La Salsa on the market. He was ditching the smoke to open up a bar in Spain. Tim had even said the same thing, though Marty would believe that when he saw it. Before he knew it, he was on Chiswick High Road and just like in the films, a black cab cruised by. He flagged it down.

The cab slowed down. Marty got in. The taxi driver was a woman. She had on a massive pair of Rayban sunglasses and a long black wig. Looked Latino of some sort.

Marty trapped his sigh and put on his best Donny Osmond smile.

'Hammersmith, please. Munster,' he grunted.

The taxi driver didn't seem to understand Marty but seemed to be able to mumble and scream at the same time. No mean feat. Marty sighed and pointed down Chiswick High Road. The taxi driver nodded.

The taxi stank of sweat, Poundland deodorant and fast food. The radio played Johnny Cash singing a Kris Kristofferson song. A normal London cab, then. But, instead of heading on down the high street toward Hammersmith, the cab did a sharp U-turn and screeched to a stop.

'Ere, what the fuck do you think you're doing?' said Marty. 'This isn't the right road.'

The driver turned and took off her sunglasses.

'Shut the fuck up. You're on a road to nowhere, sunshine, until I find out what happened to my son, Richard,' said Dusty Sanderson, waving around a Beretta.

Marty sank into his seat.

'Well,' he said. 'That's a bit of a long story, that is.'